point

CHARLES
in charge, again

A Novelization by
Elizabeth Faucher

Created by
Michael Jacobs and Barbara Weisberg,
adapted from the Charles in Charge
episode "Amityville,"
written by Michael Jacobs.

D0190079

SCHOLASTIC INC.
New York Toronto. London Auckland Sydney

ISBN 0-590-41008-3

12 11 10 9 8 7 6 5 4 3 2 1   7 8 9/8 0 1 2/9

Printed in the U.S.A.   01

First Scholastic printing, July 1987

Chapter 1

The house *looked* the same. The yard looked the same. The *street* looked the same. The car in the driveway was different, but Charles was too distracted by trying to carry his — and half of his friend Buddy's — camping gear up the front walk to notice. He nudged the front door open with one knee, then dumped everything in the entranceway with a fairly dramatic flourish.

"Hey!" he yelled. "I'm back! The hiking was great, the mountains were great, the girls were — *well*." He let his arms fall to indicate the overall excellence of the entire vacation, although he didn't seem to have an audience.

Then, he saw Lila Pembroke — the oldest of the three children he helped take care of in exchange for room and board — lying on the couch, reading. "Hey, Lila!" He stepped over the knapsack, sleeping bag, and sundry duffel bags. "How much did you miss me?"

Lila jumped up, startled. Except that it

wasn't Lila. It was — shorter. Blonder. "N-not much," she said uncertainly, holding her book up as flimsy protection. "Who are you?"

He grinned. "Lila, you've shrunk! And — your head is different. And — *now* do you see why doctors say to stay out of the sun?"

"Right." The girl kept backing away. "I'll just — Mom!" She bolted up the stairs. "Mom, come quick! There's some strange guy here!"

"Mom?" Charles said after her. In the *Pembrokes'* house? Cousins. It was probably cousins or something.

Buddy carried in his own sleeping bag and knapsack. He was wearing a cast on his left leg, holding another one in his free hand. Ordinarily, he wore beach-boy clothes — Hawaiian shirts, garish shorts, thongs, that sort of thing — to keep up his Mr. California image, but to get ready for the camping trip, he'd ordered half of the REI outdoor equipment catalog. Jeremiah Johnson image, he'd told Charles solemnly, although the effect was a lot closer to Yodeler-in-Training. He grinned at Charles.

"Forgot your cast," Buddy said.

"Uh, yeah," Charles said, taking it absent-mindedly. *Mom?* Cousin or not, there was still something strange — "Does this house look the same to you, Buddy?"

"I don't know. Sure." Buddy looked around, then shrugged. "Cleaner, maybe. But we've been out of town."

"I guess so." Charles picked up his gear, carrying it toward his bedroom. "Still, I don't — something's not right."

Buddy threw himself onto the couch, putting his feet — well, foot and cast — on the coffee table. "We've only been gone two weeks," he said. "What could not be right in two weeks?"

"Yeah, I guess." He went into his room, seeing Jason — the youngest of the Pembrokes — putting away a pile of folded shirts. "Jason, my man! Waiting for your old pal Charles to get back and tell you about his mountain-climbing adventures?"

The boy turned. A boy he had never seen before. "Well — no," the boy said. "Who are you?"

Charles just stared at him. Cousins. It had to be cousins. A *lot* of cousins.

Out in the living room, Buddy lounged on the couch, eating a piece of candy he'd found on the end table.

"Hi, Buddy," Mrs. Pembroke said, coming down the stairs.

He sat up hastily. "Hi, Mrs. Pembroke."

"What happened to your poor leg?"

"What?" He looked down. "Oh, nothing. It's a clip-on." He grinned. "See, there was a lot of competition at the campsite, and — I figured it'd give me the edge with the girls. Attract attention."

"Oh." Mrs. Pembroke smiled, too. "I had something like that when I was your age."

"A cast?"

"A padded bra," she said.

He flushed. "Mrs. *Pembroke*."

"But," she said, "when I realized I was better off being liked by someone who liked me for what I had to offer, I threw it away."

"Hunh," Buddy said, and studied his cast. "You must have had a lot more to offer than I do."

Mrs. Pembroke laughed. "Did anyone ever tell you you talk a lot, Buddy?"

"Well — almost everyone."

She laughed again, then looked more serious. "Where's Charles?"

"In his room."

"Unpacking?"

"I think so," Buddy said. "Why?"

Mrs. Pembroke bit her lip, glancing in the direction of Charles's room, on her way to the kitchen. "I just — I need to talk to him about something very important."

"Okay." Buddy found another piece of candy and unwrapped it. "I'll tell him you're looking for him."

Still in his room, Charles went over to examine the pile of folded shirts. "These, um" — he lifted what was maybe a boys' size fourteen — "don't look very much like my clothes."

The boy took the shirt away from him. "That's because they're *mine*."

"I figured," Charles said. "What's it doing on *my* shelf?"

4

"It's *my* shelf," the boy said. "What are *you* doing in *my* room?"

"*Your* room," Charles said.

"Yeah."

"If you say so." Completely rattled now, Charles went back out to the living room, very relieved to see Buddy exactly where he had left him. "Buddy, this is like a *nightmare*."

"Yeah, I hate school starting again, too," Buddy agreed, looking for more candy. "But, hey, we're sophomores now, and — "

Charles interrupted him. "Listen to me, Buddy. There's like, some kind of *Twilight Zone* thing going on here, and — "

"What are you talking about?"

"The people in this house are different," Charles said, speaking very carefully. "It may *look* like the same house, but like, *pods* or something came, and — "

"But — " Buddy shook his head. "I just saw Mrs. Pembroke. She's in the kitchen, and she wants to talk to you."

"No," Charles said. "You only *think* you saw her. If she turned around and you saw her from the front, you'd know it wasn't her."

"What?" Buddy frowned, confused, "you mean, the padded bra story?"

Too weird. This all was getting increasingly weird. Not bothering to pursue that remark, Charles headed for the kitchen, relieved to see a woman leaning inside the refrigerator.

"Boy, am I glad to see *you*," he said. "Do you know that there are people in this house who aren't supposed to be here? In the living room, in *my* room —"

The woman stood up. A woman he had never seen in his life. He stared at her, not sure if he should be amused or horrified.

"Do I know you?" she asked.

Horrified. He turned and hurried back into the living room as Mrs. Pembroke came into the kitchen through the back door.

"Was that Charles?" she asked.

"Oh, *Charles*," the woman said. "No *wonder* he was confused."

Back in the living room, Charles saw Jason — the real Jason — coming down the stairs.

"Hey, Charles, you're back," he said cheerfully.

Okay, he'd be amused. "Don't Charles *me*, you little martian shape-changer," Charles said, pointing at him. "What did you do with the Pembrokes?"

"Mountain climbing," Buddy said, when Jason looked at him for an explanation. "High altitude, thin air — *Breathe*, Charles."

Mrs. Pembroke came out from the kitchen. "There you are, Charles." She hugged him. "How was your trip?"

"Fine." Charles saw the other woman behind her. "Um, I haven't met your, uh, cousins."

Mrs. Pembroke sighed. "Actually, Charles, they're —"

6

The little boy he didn't know came out to the living room. "Have you heard he thinks my room is his room?"

"Your room *is* his room," Jason said.

The girl who had been on the couch came down the stairs. "Have you heard he called *me* a shrunken Lila?"

"Lila's the same size at our new house in Seattle," Jason said to Charles.

Charles blinked. "*What?*"

"What we should have done," the woman behind Mrs. Pembroke said, "is introduce ourselves." She put her hand out. "I'm Ellen Powell, and those are my children, Adam and Sarah. Adam, your room is upstairs."

Automatically, Charles shook her hand. "Hi." He nodded at Adam and Sarah. "Hi." He looked back at Jason. "*What?*"

"We need to talk, Charles," Mrs. Pembroke said, indicating the kitchen.

"Uh — yeah," Charles said, and nodded at the Powells. "Excuse me." He went into the kitchen after her with Buddy and Jason behind them.

Mrs. Pembroke closed the kitchen door. "I'm sorry, Charles — we tried to get in touch with you. The best we could do was some old man who lives in a cabin near the ranger station."

"Crazy Felix," Buddy said.

Mrs. Pembroke nodded. "He said he couldn't reach the climbers. I said I had important news about your life."

Charles sighed, sitting down at the table.

"He said he had important news about my *wife.* I said I didn't have a wife, and he said that that must be the news." He sighed again, resting his face in his hands.

"I'm really sorry, Charles." Mrs. Pembroke sat down across from him. "I mean, you wouldn't believe what's gone on here in the last few days." She hesitated. "There's no easy way for me to tell you this."

"My father got transferred," Jason said. "We're moving to Seattle." He smiled with very little enthusiasm. "Go, Seahawks."

"Who," Buddy said, "actually, are not a bad team. I mean, what with Largent and Warner and — "

They all looked at him.

"Krieg," he finished quietly.

Mrs. Pembroke picked up a salt shaker Charles didn't even recognize, twirling it once. "Anyway." She put it down. "We've sublet the house to the Powells — they're very nice." She looked at his unhappy expression. "We really tried to reach you."

Charles nodded. "I know; it's okay. I just — it's kind of a surprise." He managed a smile. "You know, right on top of finding out I don't have a wife, or — " He stood up. "It won't take me long to pack."

"You don't have to," Jason said.

Charles paused.

"We sublet you, too," Jason said.

"*Jason.*" Mrs. Pembroke shook her head. "All he means is that we wouldn't have considered the Powells unless they needed you the same way we did."

Charles sat back down. "Is there a Mr. Powell?"

Mrs. Pembroke nodded. "He's Commander Powell. In the Navy. He's stationed in the South Seas."

"Pretty tough commute," Charles said, and Buddy laughed.

"Actually, *Mrs.* Powell *does* have a pretty tough commute," Mrs. Pembroke said, "and — well, they'd love to have you stay here."

"Is it okay if I think about it?" Charles asked.

"Of course it is." Mrs. Pembroke got up. "Come on, Jason. Let's finish packing."

When they were gone, Charles looked over at Buddy, who was leaning against the counter, examining the contents of an Entenmann's box.

"Do you believe it?" he said.

Buddy nodded. "Kind of a rabbit punch."

"I'll say." Charles let out his breath. "What do you think I should do?"

Buddy grinned. "Stop taking vacations."

Chapter 2

"Hey, look on the bright side, Charles," Buddy said, a minute and a cupcake apiece later. "Sophomores don't have to live in dorms — we could get an apartment."

Charles thought about that. "An apartment?"

"Sure!" Buddy said. "Nothing fancy. Refrigerator, hot tub, cable. . . ."

Charles thought about it some more. "Okay."

"Really?"

"Sure," Charles said. "I mean, give me one good reason why not?"

There was a knock on the door, and Sarah Powell came in. "Excuse me, did I leave my book in here?"

Charles picked up the hardcover lying on the table. "Is this it?"

She nodded. "Thank you."

He glanced at the cover. *"Little Women."*

"Autobiography?" Buddy asked, and winked at Charles.

"*Little Women* is a classic!" Sarah said.

"Well, in *that* case," Buddy said, "I've definitely read the Cliff Notes." He grabbed another cupcake, heading for the door. "See you later, Charles — I'll go check the ads in the housing office."

Charles waved, still looking at the book cover. "I was supposed to be helping Jason with *The Red Badge of Courage*."

"I read that," Sarah said. "But not for school."

"Voluntarily?"

"It's a good book," Sarah said, her voice defensive.

"Yeah, I know; I read it. But I was forced by my teacher, Mrs. Mussolini."

Sarah just rolled her eyes and reached for the book, which Charles held out of her reach.

"What else do you read?" he asked.

"Poetry."

"Really? You have a favorite?"

"Elizabeth Barrett Browning, because she was romantic." Sarah shifted her weight. "And me."

"You write poetry?"

Sarah shrugged affirmatively.

"May I hear one?"

"Um." She shifted some more. "Could I just have my book?"

"Sure," Charles said. "I was only — " The back door flew open and he turned to see who — or what — had just come in. It was a girl maybe a year older than Sarah, with the same long blonde hair, but dressed in an outfit that would have made Madonna proud.

"Sarah," she said, "you are so lucky to have me as a sister, I should send you a bill! In *fact* — " She stopped, noticing Charles, and put on a very charming smile. "Do I know you?"

"He's Charles," Sarah said.

"*The* Charles? The Charles-who's-going-to-make-us-eat-our-vegetables Charles?" She studied him, then smiled again. "I can live with that." She refocused on Sarah. "Anyway, I'm out checking out the guys in this town and *what* do you think I find? *Only* the best-looking, most popular guy in town, who *happens* to have a brother — "

"Alexander Morgan," Charles said.

The girl looked at him. "How did you know?"

Charles shrugged. "Best-looking junior high guy in town."

"Oh," the girl said. "Anyway, Sarah, you and I are having a soda with the Morgans this very afternoon, so comb your hair, change your clothes, and burn the book!" She pushed the door to the living room open, pausing only to look back at Charles. "I don't *do* squash."

"Got it," Charles said, as the door swung shut.

"That's my sister, Jamie," Sarah said. "You like her better than me, right?"

"Well, I — "

Sarah nodded. "I knew you did." She

headed for the living room, Charles going after her.

"I don't like her better than you," he said. "I mean — I hardly know you. And I know her even less."

"Not for long," Sarah said. "Jamie knows how to get popular."

"What's going on?" Mrs. Powell asked, carrying one of the Pembrokes' suitcases downstairs.

He wasn't going to start. He was moving to an apartment with Buddy, and there was no reason to — "Nothing, Mrs. Powell," he said aloud. "I'm not involved. I *don't* get involved in this sort of thing anymore." Except that Sarah looked pretty sad, and it really wouldn't kill him to — "Look," he said to her. "It sounds to me like she's just trying to get you popular, too."

"But I'm not *ready*," Sarah said.

"To have a Coke with someone?"

"To be *popular*."

Mrs. Pembroke came downstairs with Jason, both of them lugging suitcases. "Did you check your closet?" she was asking.

"Six hundred times," Jason said.

"Well — go check it again," she said.

Sarah tapped Charles on the arm to get his attention. "I said, do you know what happens when you get popular too fast?"

"Academy awards?" he guessed. "Gold records? Vegas twelve weeks a year?"

"You burn out. You *peak*." She put her

hand to her chest. "*I* want to endure. Like Elizabeth Barrett Browning and —"

"Louisa May Alcott?" Charles said.

"Well — yeah. I mean, they're both still popular."

"They're also both *dead*."

Sarah turned, looking for her mother. "Mom, Charles thinks it's important to my life that I meet boys."

"People," Charles said. "I said, people. I think she's new in town, and this is a perfect chance to make some friends."

Mrs. Powell shrugged. "What's wrong with that, Sarah?"

"Everything!" Sarah said. "I don't know how to meet people I don't know."

"Those are the only people you *can* meet," Charles pointed out.

Jason opened the front door to carry his suitcase out, just as Buddy was lifting his hand to knock. "Hi, Buddy," he said. "Want to trade lives?"

"Can you show me how?" Sarah asked Charles. "How to make friends, I mean?"

"Well — see, the first thing — " Charles stopped, seeing Buddy. "No. No, I can't. It's my absolute new policy not to get involved in any more kids' lives."

"Good move, Charles," Buddy said. "Because this is *our* year." He came over, draping his arm around Charles's shoulder and steering him away from everyone else. "I met two *great* girls who were putting up an ad in Housing, and if they like us, they're going to recommend us as new tenants."

"But — they don't know us."

Buddy nodded. *"That's* why they're waiting over at Sid's for us to buy them a pizza."

Charles shook his head. "I can't — I want to drive the Pembrokes to the airport."

"We're *hitching* cross-country," Jason said.

"Jason." Mrs. Pembroke sounded tired. "Charles, thank you, but we're really all set. We called a cab."

"Yeah, but — I could *drive* the cab," Charles said.

A horn beeped outside and Jason went to the front door to look. "It's here," he said.

Charles and Mrs. Pembroke looked at each other.

"Well," Charles said.

Mrs. Pembroke hugged him. "We're really going to miss you, Charles."

"Me, too," he said.

As Buddy helped Mrs. Pembroke out with the suitcases, Charles looked at Jason. "It's going to be hard growing up without you," Charles said.

Jason hugged him, fast, and ran out.

"Come on, pal," Buddy said, back from the cab. "Let's go meet those girls. Let's meet our new life!"

Charles nodded, waving as the cab pulled away. "Right." He smiled awkwardly at Sarah and Mrs. Pembroke. "Well, um, it was very nice to have — "

"You're going somewhere to meet new people?" Sarah asked.

"Well — yeah."

"Girls?"

"Yeah," he said.

"Charles," Buddy said, his voice holding a warning.

"Do you mind if I come watch?" Sarah asked.

"Whoa!" Buddy said, stepping between them. "Time-out!" He put his hands on Charles's shoulders. *"No.* Do you hear me? *No.* That's over now, you understand? No more children, okay? Your *new* life is out that door, and if you know what's good for you, you'll follow me through it." He nodded politely at the Powells. "It was nice to have met you."

Adam came out of Charles's room with a large stack of clothes. "Charles, you can have your room back — I got all my stuff out."

"No, Charles," Buddy said from the front door.

Mrs. Powell moved to take some of the clothes from Adam, the stack teetering. "Charles, you have my permission to take Sarah with you as long as you have her back before dinner."

"I'm sorry," Buddy said, "but Charles does not have *my* permission to bring Sarah, and — "

"Besides," Jamie said, suddenly standing at the top of the staircase. "What can Charles teach Sarah about meeting people that I can't? When *I* get through with her, she's going to be just like me!"

Sarah groaned, and before Charles could say anything, Buddy jumped between them again.

"Charles, I smell involvement here," he said urgently. "Involvement permeates this house like a skunk. It's — it's *Amityville*, Charles."

Charles looked at Buddy, looked at Sarah, looked back at Buddy. "I'm sorry," he said. "I'm — I'm really sorry." Turning before he could see Sarah's disappointment, he followed Buddy out of the house.

Sarah stared after him. "He left without me, Mom."

Mrs. Powell patted her on the shoulder. "He's allowed, Sarah. He doesn't have any obligation to us."

"But — I asked him nicely, didn't I?"

Mrs. Powell smiled. "Of course you did."

"Well, then — what's his problem?"

"I don't know." Mrs. Powell picked up the candy wrappers Buddy had left on the coffee table, dropping them in the fireplace. "I guess after all of the glowing reports we got from the Pembrokes, we expected something more than just a regular nice guy."

"Well, *I* don't think he's nice at all," Sarah said. "A *nice* guy would have let me come with him."

"Let a thirteen-year-old come along on a date? Come on, Sarah."

"Yeah, well, he shouldn't have *pretended* to be nice if he wasn't."

"Oh, Sarah, I'm sure he didn't mean — "

"No!" They heard Buddy yelling from outside. "Charles, don't! Charles — "

The front door opened, and Charles came back in, motioning for Sarah to come with him.

"Aw, *Charles*," Buddy called out.

Sarah looked at her mother, who smiled, and nodded for her to go with him.

"Okay," Sarah said, going to the door. "The jury's still out on him."

Chapter 3

Charles was about to close the door behind them when a tall, angry man with white hair strode up the walk, sending the three of them back inside.

"Just *where*," he said, "do you boys think you're taking my little granddaughter?"

"Uh, well," Charles said, looking at Mrs. Powell for help.

"This is Charles, Dad," she said. "The young man the Pembrokes told us so much about. And boys, this is Walter Powell, my father-in-law."

"United States Navy," Mr. Powell said, saluting them. "Retired." He frowned at Charles. "So you're the famous Charles, eh?"

"Famous, sir?" Charles said.

"Those Pembrokes went on about you like you were Admiral Rickover." Mr. Powell shook his head, apparently not impressed by what he was seeing.

Buddy nudged Charles. "Admiral who?"

Mr. Powell frowned at *both* of them. "Friend of yours, Charles?"

"Uh, yes, sir," Charles said, standing straighter than usual. "Buddy Lembeck, sir."

"I see." Mr. Powell examined him, hands behind his back. "And how is it, *Mr.* Lembeck, that you are not acquainted with the infrastructure of your country's military?"

"Hey, look," Buddy said, shrugging, "it's all I can do to meet women."

"I see." Mr. Powell did not crack a smile. "And I suppose you call yourself an American."

"Actually," Buddy started, "my great-grandparents were — "

"Name one military victory!" Mr. Powell ordered.

Buddy grinned. "Mary Louise — "

"We really have to be going," Charles cut him off. "It was nice to meet you, sir, and — "

"Oh, no, you don't!" Mr. Powell pulled Sarah back. "My granddaughter isn't going *anywhere* with you two college deferments."

Yes, an off-campus apartment was sounding better and better. "Sir," Charles said calmly, "Sarah wasn't drafted to go on this mission, she enlisted. And, it'll be our pleasure to show her a little bit of her new town and buy her a piece of pizza."

Mr. Powell didn't release her. "I am more than capable of showing my granddaughter around myself — *plus*, I am not sure that you're showing the proper respect for your new employer!"

"You're not my employer, sir. I'm just doing a favor for a new friend." Charles ushered both Sarah and Buddy over to the door. "Otherwise, I'm not involved."

The door closed before Mr. Powell could protest. He turned to his daughter-in-law. "Ellen, how can you allow — "

"You heard him, Dad," Mrs. Powell said. "He's not involved."

"But — that is — "

The kitchen door was already swinging shut behind her.

Sid's Pizza Parlour was the main Crawford College hangout. The crusts were thin, the tomato sauce was thick, and the jukebox was *great*. It was fairly crowded for mid-afternoon, and Buddy looked around for the girls they were meeting.

"I'll check the place out, Charles," he said. "See if they've gotten here yet. Hey, Sid," he said to the guy behind the counter.

Sid stopped slicing onions. "Hey, Buddy. Where's — hey, Charles."

"Hi, Sid." Charles leaned over the counter. "I'm going to make you a deal, okay?"

Sid grinned, wiping his hands on his apron. "Unh-hunh."

"I owe you money, right?"

"Right," Sid said.

"Well, how about you make us a pizza, and I'll owe you *more* money. How's that?"

"You'd do that for me, Charles? What a guy." Sid shook his head.

"Think of it as one small step — "

"Yeah, yeah, yeah," Sid said, reaching for a ball of dough. "But only," he smiled at Sarah, "because you're finally keeping classy company."

Buddy hadn't come back yet, so Charles went over to the jukebox, Sarah behind him.

"How are you going to act with the girls?" she asked.

He punched in B105, Otis Redding, "The Dock of the Bay." "Like myself," he said. "The main thing when you meet new people is to just be yourself."

"Jamie says just being myself is what keeps me from being popular."

He laughed, punching in R67. Huey Lewis, "The Heart of Rock and Roll." "Do you agree with her?"

"No," Sarah said slowly, "but I'm not popular."

"It's a state of mind, more than anything else." He checked his pockets for another quarter. "I mean, when I was in junior high — "

"Hey, Charles!" Across the restaurant, Buddy put his thumb and forefinger in his mouth, and gave out a piercing whistle. "Over here!"

"What are you going to say to them?" Sarah asked, as they walked over to the table. "I mean, how do you start? How do you pace yourself?"

"I don't know," he said. "Conversations usually find their own pace."

The girls were *very* beautiful. In a blatant sort of way. Which was one of his favorite ways. Long, teased blonde hair; big smiles; lots of lip gloss.

"Hi, there," he said, and smiled *his* most charming smile.

"*Hi*, there," the girl with the blondest hair said. "I'm Patti, and that's Heidi." She touched the seat next to her. "Sit down, gorgeous."

"This, for example, looks like a fast-paced conversation," Charles said to Sarah, motioning for her to sit down, too. "This is my friend, Sarah."

"Hi," Patti said, still looking at Charles. "How did you make such a good-looking friend?"

"Um, I moved," Sarah said, uncertainly.

"There you go!" Patti hit the table lightly. "A girl after my own heart." She put her arm on Charles's shoulder. "So. How's it going?"

He smiled back at her. "*Very* fast-paced," he said to Sarah.

Back at the house, Mr. Powell was still blustering as his daughter-in-law got dinner ready.

"And just *what* did he mean when he said I wasn't his employer?" he asked.

Mrs. Powell shrugged, shaping a meatloaf. "He means he hasn't decided whether he wants to be employed or not, Dad."

"Well." He folded his arms. "There'd be

no decision for him if you'd quit working and raise your children."

She sighed. "I *like* working. And my children have been raised very well up to now, wouldn't you say?"

Jamie came in from the living room, her hair wildly mousséd, wearing an outfit so tight that it would have *embarrassed* Madonna. "How do I look?" she asked, particularly indicating the leopard-print pants.

"Wash your face and burn those clothes," Mrs. Powell said.

"What?" Jamie said. "You think the mascara's a little much?"

"*Now*," her mother said, and Jamie left. Quickly. Mrs. Powell didn't look at her father-in-law. "I know, I know, don't say it."

"No, I understand," Mr. Powell said. "With my son off on manuevers. . . . Well, it's hard for one parent to be on the lookout all the time."

"That's why we need someone like Charles."

"*That's* why I've decided to stop working at the surplus store and raise them myself," he said.

"No!" Mrs. Powell said, then lowered her voice. "I mean, no. I mean — it's very generous, but I really don't — I mean, you have your own life, and I — "

"You *like* this Charles character, don't you," Mr. Powell said, frowning.

"Yes," she said. "And Sarah likes him, and I trust her judgment." She glanced in the direction Jamie had gone. "And I think he just might be a very good influence."

Sid had brought their pizza over, and Patti had decided to feed Charles his, with the others looking on in some fascination.

"You see, Sarah?" Charles said, his voice only a little weak. "Meeting new people can be a lot of fun."

Sarah leaned forward on her elbows. "Could I ask you girls something?"

"Sure," Heidi said, tossing her hair back. "Fire away."

"Are you being yourselves?"

Patti tossed her hair, too. "What do you mean?"

"I mean, have you always been like this?"

"Well, of *course*," Heidi said, with what could only be described as a merry laugh.

"No." Patti looked almost serious. "Not me. You know what I was when I was your age?"

"Brunette," Sarah guessed.

Patti laughed. Sunnily. "*And* I wore glasses, and I used to read *poetry*." She shuddered. "Can you imagine?"

"Then, how did you get to be so — " Sarah hesitated. "Well, so — "

"Much fun?" Patti said. "Well, I met Heidi! Joined the sorority, bought new clothes, and makeup, and — "

"Do you still read poetry?" Sarah asked.

"Well — " Patti had to think. "Limericks. Sometimes."

"Oh, yeah?" Buddy said. "Let's hear one."

Patti smiled voluptuously. It took practice, that smile. "There was a young girl from — "

Anticipating a rhyme that would be seamy at best, Charles jumped up, pulling Sarah along with him. "Uh, catch you later, guys, okay?" he said.

"Thank you, Charles," Sarah whispered.

He grinned, opening the door for her. "Don't mention it."

Chapter 4

When Charles and Sarah got back to the house, Jamie was waiting for them, pacing up and down in the living room. She stopped when she saw them come in.

"It's about time," she said. "I don't know if the Morgans are still waiting — even for me! Let's go!"

Sarah shook her head, sitting down on the couch. "I don't want to meet any boys."

Jamie stopped, halfway to the door. "*What?*"

Charles sat down on the couch, too. "Just what she said, Jamie. She's not ready yet. It's her decision."

Jamie put her hands on her hips. "Thank you, Michael Landon."

"Look," Sarah said, "I don't see why you can't wait until school starts to meet people, anyway."

Jamie turned toward the kitchen. "Mom!"

Mrs. Powell came out, followed by their grandfather.

"What is it?" she asked.

Jamie indicated Charles. "He's rubbing off on her the wrong way!"

"Just what sort of problem have you caused, young man?" Mr. Powell wanted to know.

"No problem," Charles said, nodding for Buddy — who had just shown up at the front door — to come in. "Everything's under control." He smiled at Jamie. "Your sister's right — you don't have to run to meet boys. Let them run to meet *you*."

"You're not my boss," Jamie said, not smiling back. "You don't work here."

"Yes, he does," Sarah said.

Everyone looked at her.

"He does?" Mrs. Powell said.

"He most certainly — " Mr. Powell started.

Sarah moved over next to Charles. "*Please?*"

"The apartment!" Buddy said, waving to get his attention. "The girls said it's ours if we want it!"

Charles looked at Sarah, looked at Buddy, then sighed. "Sorry, Buddy."

Buddy sighed, too. "No, I expected it." He sighed again. "Dorms aren't so bad."

No one said anything for a minute.

"Well." Mrs. Powell broke the silence. "Dinner's almost ready. Buddy, I'll set a place for you."

"Thank you, Mrs. Powell," Buddy said,

already over his disappointment and back to being charming. "And may I say, it smells delicious."

"Wait," Adam said, having come downstairs during all of the commotion. "What about Charles?"

"His place is *already* set." Mrs. Powell disappeared into the kitchen. Adam followed.

"It *is*?" Mr. Powell said. "You mean to say — you're going to employ this, this — " He frowned at Charles. "I'm not happy about this."

Charles couldn't think of any sort of response to that, so he just shrugged pleasantly.

"I'll have my eye on you," Mr. Powell said, and went into the kitchen.

Jamie was still shaking her head over missing the meeting with the Morgan boys. "I don't know, Sarah, I don't know. We might've met a couple of nice boys."

Sarah smiled at Charles and Buddy. "We *did*, Jamie."

"Girls?" Mrs. Powell called from the kitchen. "Could you come in here and give me a hand, please?"

"I'm sorry," Charles said to Buddy. "I didn't mean to mess up your plans."

Buddy shook his head. "No, I knew you'd do this."

Charles glanced at the kitchen. "I have to save Sarah from Jamie." He grinned. "I have to save *Jamie* from Jamie."

"Too bad about those girls, though," Buddy said. "I wouldn't've minded spending a little more time with them."

"We will," Charles said.

"Hunh?"

"I made us a date. Their apartment. Nine o'clock."

"You did?"

Charles nodded.

"All right!" Buddy said. "Those girls were *hot*!"

Charles grinned. "Can't save *everyone*."

He was almost asleep that night when he heard his bedroom door open.

"It's okay," Adam whispered, coming inside. "He's asleep."

"I really don't think —" Sarah started.

"Come on." Jamie pushed her the rest of the way into the room. "Let's see what we've got here."

Aware of them standing by the bed, watching to make sure he was asleep, Charles managed an artistic turn or two. When he'd been about ten, trying to get out of school or something, his parents had always known he was faking because, supposedly asleep, he would lie absolutely still. He'd finally figured out that moving around a little made the act more convincing.

"He's going to teach me how to throw a knuckleball," Adam was saying.

Probably not. He had a pretty good curve, though.

"*And* how to drive a car," Adam said.

In three or four *years*, maybe.

"We're going to read all the classics together," Sarah said happily.

No *Beowulf*. No *Ivanhoe*, either.

"He's going to do my math homework," Jamie said, "clean my room — this is great. We *own* this guy. He has to do whatever we — "

This was getting out of hand, maybe.

"Go to bed," he said, making his voice extra stern.

They ran out of the room, practically falling over each other, and he smiled as he heard them running up the stairs.

Maybe this *was* going to work out.

Chapter 5

Charles woke up early the next morning, the confidence of the night before having faded into "What am I doing there, and is it too late to get out of it?" But, instead of lying in bed worrying, he got dressed and went out to the kitchen to see about breakfast. Should he cook something for everyone? He generally had for the Pembrokes. It had been a little rocky at first, but after a year with them, he had gotten to be an *adequate* cook — with a few glaring exceptions.

Well, he'd go ahead and make something, and even if they didn't want it, they would know that his heart was in the right place. Eggs with onions and peppers and whatever else was in the refrigerator? But maybe the kids were the type who hated vegetables — hadn't Jamie said something about squash? — so maybe he should just play it safe and — French toast. Just about everyone liked French toast.

He got out the bread, milk, eggs, and cinnamon, all of which were in slightly different places than the Pembrokes had kept them. A new family. Was he really up for a new family? Maybe Buddy was right, and they should just get an apartment together, start new — he'd already made his decision. He might not be *sure* about it, but he couldn't go around changing his mind. He'd been nervous when he'd started living with the Pembrokes, too, and *that* had worked out all right.

He took out a package of bacon, a frying pan, a bowl, an eggbeater, and a cookie sheet. He had learned by experience that broiling bacon in the oven was a lot better than frying it. It didn't burn or shrink as much that way. He turned on the oven, cracked six eggs into the bowl, and started beating them.

Jamie came in, wearing a royal-blue miniskirt made of some sort of shiny fabric, two differently ripped T-shirts bloused over a skinny leather belt, and a number of clunky red, blue, and yellow bracelets on each arm.

" 'Morning," Charles said cheerfully.

"Uh, 'morning," she said, tying her hair up with an electric-blue scarf.

He grinned. "Take MTV pretty seriously, do you?"

"It's called style," she said.

"You must have been pretty upset about Wham! breaking up."

"*You're* probably still upset about the Doobie Brothers," she said.

He laughed, although, actually, she had a point.

She leaned over the bowl to see what he was doing. "You *cook?*"

He sprinkled some more cinnamon in, along with some nutmeg. "Sure."

"Boys don't *cook,"* she said.

He laughed. "Somewhere, Phyllis Schlafly just smiled."

Jamie smiled a little, too. "Well, what is it, a *quiche?*"

"French toast," he said.

"Oh. Well, I usually just have coffee."

"Unh-hunh," he said, amused.

She sat down at the table, drumming on it with one hand, and looking at her, it suddenly occurred to him that her being aggressive was really just a way of being nervous.

"So." He put some butter in the frying pan. "How do you feel about moving?"

"Piece of cake," she said, too quickly. *"Speaking* of which — " She went over to the counter where there was yet another Entenmann's box.

"No cake for breakfast," Charles said before she could open it.

She didn't pause. "You can't tell me what to do. You work for *us.*"

"I work for your *mother.*"

"Yeah, well." She turned. "Let's get some ground rules straight here. A, you don't tell me what to do. B, you have to — "

"Here's my ground rule," he said. *"You* don't tell *me* what to do, okay?"

She was about to argue, but instead, opened the cupboard, taking down a coffee mug and a jar of instant coffee.

"If you make it," he said, "you have to drink it."

She scowled at him, but poured herself a glass of orange juice, putting the coffee away. "I don't know why they all think you're so nice."

The butter in the pan had melted — over very low heat so it wouldn't brown — and he put two pieces of egg-soaked bread in. "I don't know," he said. "Low standards, I guess."

"I mean, you're *cute* enough," she said, "but how come you don't want to live in a dorm?"

He opened drawers, looking for a spatula. "Well, *last* year, I didn't have any choice. My financial aid got all mixed up, the Pembrokes offered me the job, and — well, it was either that, or don't go to school."

"Did you get financial aid this year?"

He finally found the spatula and checked the toast to see if it was browning. Not yet. "I still haven't heard, but I would have stayed with the Pembrokes, anyway."

"Wouldn't you rather be in a dorm?"

Now it was brown enough. He flipped both pieces. "In some ways, sure." He put two more pieces of bread into the egg mixture to soak. "But, in others — well, I was an only child, so it's nice to be around a big family. See what it's like."

"Oh." She thought about that. "What if you don't like *us*?"

He shrugged, checking the bacon. "I'll worry about that if it happens."

"Do you expect it to?"

He grinned. "No."

"Oh." She thought about that, too. "I guess you like Sarah a lot better than me."

"No," he said. "Why?"

"Well, the Pembrokes said you were really smart, and she is, too, and — well, you *did* go out with her yesterday."

He laughed. "She thinks I like *you* better."

"Yeah, right," Jamie said. "Why?"

"Oh, because you're pretty and popular and all of the things she wants to be."

Jamie shook her head. "She'd rather have good grades. I mean, if she had to choose."

"I don't know." Charles put the cooked French toast on a plate, covering it with a bowl to keep it warm. "Maybe."

Jamie watched him put two more pieces in the pan. "I don't get good grades."

"Okay," he said.

"I don't even *try*."

He nodded, turning to pay attention to what she was saying.

"See" — she looked embarrassed — "if I *tried*, I might *get* good grades, but they might not be *as* good. As hers, I mean." She folded her arms. "This way I'm, like, an unknown quantity. I mean, they don't know if I'm smart or *not*."

"They probably figure you are," he said. "Just as they think she's pretty."

"Well, anyway." She looked even more embarrassed. "Don't tell anyone I told you that."

"Okay, but — "

"Please don't give me the 'It's not a contest, and we don't compare you with your sister and brother' speech," she said.

He stopped, having been about to launch into that sort of speech. "Okay," he said, and flipped the French toast. He poured himself some orange juice. "How *do* you feel about moving?"

She shrugged. "Hey, no sweat — we do it all the time."

"All over the place?"

"Well, Navy bases are *usually* near the ocean," she said.

He grinned. "Probably so."

"We've been the new kids, like, *sixteen* times."

He nodded. "I guess you get used to having to make friends fast."

"Well — yeah," she said. "Kind of. I mean, I guess my father's a really good leader because they're always moving him around to shape up units."

"How long is he going to be away?"

Jamie shrugged. "I don't know, it's always different. Sarah and Adam and I had to look at a globe to even figure out where the South Seas *are*." She frowned. "They're big." She shook her head. "Anyway, we aren't even sure where they're going to want him to be, although he's pretty sure they'll let him work out of Washington or Bethesda or something; and Mom wants the three of us to live in a regular house for a while, and go to regular school and all."

Charles nodded, taking the bacon out of the oven.

"I kind of like it better on base," Jamie said. "I mean, there, *everyone's* a Navy brat, so they all know what it's like."

"Moving around so much, you must have gotten to meet a lot of interesting people," Charles guessed.

"Yeah, but you don't get to know them *well*. I mean, you always figure you're going to move soon, anyway."

Charles nodded, locating and putting out the maple syrup, then serving Jamie. "It sounds fun in some ways, though. I mean, going away to school is the first chance I've had to get to know a lot of different kinds of people."

"Like your friend, Surfer-Boy?"

"Yeah," Charles said, laughing. "Like my friend, Buddy." He served his own breakfast and sat down across from her since it didn't look as though anyone else was going to get up any time soon.

"It's funny," Jamie said, pouring some syrup on her French toast. "I *never* talk to people like this. I mean, serious and all."

"Don't worry," Charles said. "I won't tell anyone."

She smiled. "Maybe I *do* like you a little."

He smiled back. "That can be our secret, too."

They were just finishing breakfast when Mr. Powell, slightly winded, wearing a navy blue sweat suit, came in through the back door.

"Here now," he said. "What's all this?"

"Breakfast, Grandpa," Jamie said. "Charles made it."

Mr. Powell frowned. "*I* usually make breakfast for the family. Up with the birds, you know."

Charles nodded. "I usually cooked it for the Pembrokes, sir. I guess I'm still in the habit."

"Well, at least you're an early riser." Mr. Powell patted Jamie on the head. "Good morning, pumpkin. Where are those other grandchildren of mine?"

"Sleeping."

"Don't they know this is the shank of the morning?" Mr. Powell asked, shaking his head in possibly mock dismay.

"Should I go wake them up?" Jamie asked, already halfway to her feet.

"Certainly," Mr. Powell said. "Tell them time's a-wasting, and breakfast's getting cold."

Jamie grinned. "Can I tell them they're lazy?"

"Make sure you *do*," Mr. Powell said, and she left the room.

Charles got up to reheat the frying pan. "Can I interest you in some French toast, sir?"

Mr. Powell nodded, turning on the kettle for coffee. "Sounds capital," he said.

Charles broke a few more eggs into the bowl, beating them up. "Do you jog, sir?" he asked, searching for a conversation topic.

"Race-walk," Mr. Powell said. "Man my age looks foolish trying to run around like a youngster. You a runner?"

"Sometimes," Charles said, grating more nutmeg. "I was into it in high school, but now I'm more likely to play some basketball with Buddy and guys at school, or touch football or something."

"What *about* that Buddy?" Mr. Powell asked. "He as goofy as he seems?"

Charles laughed. "No. He's just — enthusiastic."

"So, what's wrong with you two young men that you aren't R.O.T.C.?"

Charles laughed again, picturing that. "*Buddy*? I don't know, sir. I think he might be a little disruptive."

"Well, what about you? You seem a likely enough candidate."

"I, uh" — tact was indicated here — "I spend a lot of time studying, sir."

"Builds character, military training does," Mr. Powell said, getting up to fix his coffee now that the water was boiling.

"I'm sure it does, sir," Charles said. "I just — what with my job here, and my studies, I really don't — "

"Well, what are you going to do with yourself, then?" Mr. Powell wanted to know, sitting back down. Charles noticed how good his posture was. "When you get out."

What *was* he going to do with himself? "I don't know, sir."

"What are you studying?"

"Liberal arts, sir."

Mr. Powell frowned. "What does *that* mean?"

Charles grinned. "It means I can't make up my mind, so I study all kinds of things."

"Such as?"

"Well, I haven't registered yet for this semester, but things like political science and history and English lit and — "

"What's wrong with *American* lit?" Mr. Powell asked.

Charles put on more French toast. "I took it last semester, sir."

"Good for you," Mr. Powell said. "Take some more of it."

"Yes, sir. I'm sure I will."

Mr. Powell nodded. "Good for you. What about that Buddy character?"

Mr. Powell was going to *love* this. "Actually, sir, he asks girls he thinks are pretty what *they're* taking, then he signs up."

"Sounds like an incipient sailor to *me*," Mr. Powell said.

Charles laughed. "I'll tell him you said so."

"I'll tell him myself. Gather he hangs around a lot."

"As a rule," Charles said.

"Seems harmless enough?" Mr. Powell said, his voice lifting slightly with the last word.

Charles nodded. "Yeah, he's harmless."

There was the sound of at least three pairs of feet on the stairs, and they both looked in the direction of the living room.

"Hope you have enough toast there," Mr. Powell said.

"Yes, sir," Charles said, and grinned. "Enough to feed an army."

Chapter 6

In his room later, going over the course registration book yet again to try and decide what he wanted to take, Charles heard someone at the door.

"Come in," he said, not getting up from his desk.

Adam opened the door, staying behind the threshold. "Are you busy?"

Charles turned. "No, not at all. Come on in."

"You *look* busy."

Charles put the book down. "Just trying to figure out what I'm going to take this fall. What are you up to today?"

Adam shrugged, still behind the threshold.

"Well, what's everyone else up to?"

Adam made a face. "Shopping. For school junk and all."

"You aren't getting any junk this year?"

"Not if *I* can help it," Adam said.

"Your grandfather going shopping, too?"

Adam shook his head. "He works at, like, a surplus store."

"Army/Navy?"

Adam relaxed enough to smile. "Well, yeah." He shifted his weight. "Is, like, your friend coming over?"

"Probably, yeah."

"And you'll hang out with him?"

"Probably. What are *you* going to do?"

"I don't know." Adam kicked at the floor, not really looking at him. "I don't know anyone around here, so there's not, like, much to do."

"You'll know lots of people once school starts."

Adam nodded pessimistically.

"Well, I'll tell you," Charles said. "There's this arcade I used to go to with Jason and his brother. How about you and Buddy and I go there and waste some quarters?"

Adam's expression brightened, but he didn't quite look up. "Will your friend mind? Having me along, I mean?"

"Of course not."

"He didn't, um, seem too happy when Sarah went with you guys yesterday."

Charles laughed. "We were meeting *girls*, Adam. Buddy turns into a crazy man when girls're involved, but he didn't really mind."

"Will there be girls at the arcade?"

Charles laughed again. "With luck."

The arcade was very crowded, but the girls either seemed to have dates, or be under twelve. Adam, had he been so inclined, could probably have done very well.

"What do you want to play first?" Adam was asking.

Charles glanced around at the machines. "It's your call."

"Do they have — Galaga?"

Charles nodded, pointing.

"You're probably a record-breaker on this," Buddy guessed as they crossed over to the machine.

"I've only played it a few times," Adam said, with the modest shrug of an eleven-year-old who practically *owns* the game.

Charles dropped two quarters in, pressing the two players button. "You want to play him, Buddy?"

"This, um, this isn't one of my best games," Buddy said.

"We've been coming here for a year, and we've yet to find *any* of his best games," Charles said to Adam. "You want to go first?"

"No, you can," Adam said, moving to the side of the machine to watch.

Charles shrugged, and took command of his first ship, firing at the first group of little bombers, or whatever they were supposed to be, that came out. He got them all, and the next batch was a little faster.

"Hey, look out!" Buddy said, as bombs fell in slow diagonals.

Charles dogged them easily, still shooting. "I see them, I see them."

"Yeah, but — watch it!"

"Can't take this guy anywhere," Charles said to Adam, who laughed. That lapse of concentration was, however, a mistake, as he promptly lost his ship.

"You shot a lot of them," Adam said.

"Unh-hunh," Charles said, surrendering the machine for Adam's turn.

By the time Adam had deftly fired his way through the sixth wave, Charles and Buddy were watching with their arms folded.

"Kids," Buddy said. "Never fails that kids are great at these."

"If you *really* want to be depressed," Charles said, "go *skiing* with a kid sometime."

Adam fired his way to the seventh screen. "It's, um, it's really just luck."

"Unh-hunh," Charles said.

"Sure," Buddy said.

When Adam had finally finished — Charles having gone through his allotment of ships much less admirably — they waited for him to enter his initials as the third highest scorer in the history of that particular machine.

"Well, one thing's for sure," Buddy said. "You definitely get your quarter's worth." He looked around the crowded arcade. "I don't know, maybe I should just go find myself Pac-Man and leave it at that."

Charles shook his head. "Pac-Man's for lightweights."

"Oh, yeah?" Buddy said. "You want me to

spread it around that I caught you playing the trivia machine once?"

"Don't feel bad, Charles," Adam said. "One time, we were at this Howard Johnson's, and Sarah and I played Pong."

"Oooh." Buddy winced. "Better keep that to yourself, kid."

"Hey, over there!" Charles pointed at Centipede. "*There's* a game I've put some initials on."

"You know what I like?" Buddy said as they walked over. "The *Star Wars* game where you get to climb into the capsule and all, and he keeps telling you" — Buddy put on an Alec Guinness voice — " 'Use the Force, Luke. The Force is with you.' I mean" — he spoke in his normal voice — "most of these other games, you have to spend at least a dollar before you even figure out what's going *on*."

"Charles, can I go try that one?" Adam pointed at what appeared to be an inordinately complicated spaceship game.

"Sure." Charles gave him four quarters. "Go crazy."

"Seems like a nice kid," Buddy said when he was gone.

Charles nodded, dropping two quarters into Centipede. "They're all nice."

"Even the old guy?"

Charles nodded again, firing at the centipede at the top of the screen. "He's just sort of — set in his ways."

"Does he make them do pushups in the morning and all?"

Charles laughed. "No. He definitely wants them to rise and shine, though."

"He'll probably try to make you join up," Buddy said. "Especially — hey, look out for that crab!"

Charles shot it for six hundred points. "It's not a crab, it's a spider."

"No way — spiders have eight legs."

"It's a game, Buddy. It's supposed to be — evocative."

"Yeah, well, it *looks* like — there's another!"

Charles shot it. "I've played this game a million times, Buddy."

"I know, I know," Buddy said. "Just trying to help."

Charles shot away the last of the centipedes, moving to the next level. "He does think we ought to be in R.O.T.C."

"Oh, yeah, right," Buddy said. "March around all afternoon with, like, a stick on my shoulder?"

Charles nodded, firing like crazy with his left hand, positioning his shooter with the rotating ball under his right hand.

"Oh, hit that thing," Buddy said, as the first inchworm moved across the screen. "It's worth a lot."

"A thousand," Charles said, managing to shoot it just as it was moving off the edge of the screen.

Buddy watched him play for another couple of minutes. "Hey, wait a minute," he said suddenly. "You've been playing for a long time — aren't I ever going to get a turn?"

"You're *supposed* to play as long as you can, Buddy." Charles shot into the next level. "That's the point."

"Yeah, but I'm getting really bored."

"That doesn't mean it's fair to try and screw me up."

Buddy shrugged. "If you were really concentrating, you'd be able to tune me out."

Charles looked over. "I *am* concentrating."

"Just trying to be helpful."

"Just trying to get me to — " Charles sighed, having been distracted just enough to lose his turn. "You did that on purpose."

Buddy grinned. "Who, me?" He moved in for his turn. "Now, *watch* a master at work."

"Okay," Charles said, "but he's all the way over there."

"Ha," Buddy said, firing wildly at anything that moved on the screen. "Now see, the trick is to be very light and quick with the left hand, and very smooth and — " He stopped, his shooter having already exploded.

"I think it's my turn," Charles said.

Buddy stepped aside. "What a dumb game."

Charles laughed.

"Well, it is."

"What a good sport," Charles said, shooting away.

"How come I live in a dorm and waste a lot of time hanging around the game room, and *you're* better than I am at the stupid things?" Buddy asked.

"I don't know." Bunches of earwigs and ladybugs and inchworms and things were zipping around the screen, and Charles tried to keep them all in his frame of vision, tried to shoot without panic. "One of life's little mysteries, I guess."

"Yeah." Buddy yawned. "So, you think we should give Patti and Heidi a call tonight?"

The spiders were *very* fast now, and Charles barely managed to manuever out of the way. "They were — well, a little shallow, don't you think?"

"They're both really pretty though."

"Yeah, I know. I just — " Charles struggled to concentrate on what he was doing. "Just didn't seem like a match made in heaven, somehow."

"So, who needs that?" Buddy asked. "We're young. We're in our prime."

"You mean, it's all downhill from here?"

Buddy looked worried. "I hope not. That'd be really — "

Charles sighed as he lost his turn again and moved aside.

Buddy took over the controls. "Kind of like walking and chewing gum, hunh? I mean, if you can't talk and play at the same time, you really shouldn't — " One of the spiders blew away his defender.

Charles grinned at him. "You were saying?"

Buddy lifted his hands from the controls. "Nothing."

Charles ended up with a respectable, if not record-breaking, score, while Buddy's last turn was as disastrous as his first two.

"You going to kick it?" Charles asked, indicating the machine.

"No, too many people around." His expression brightened. "Hey, I know!"

"What?"

"Let's find some good, honest pinball. *That* I can do."

"Since when?"

"Since always," Buddy said. "That was *me* The Who meant."

Adam came over, finished with his game. "Hi."

"How'd you do?" Charles asked.

Adam shrugged, but Charles detected the tiny note of telltale modesty. "What about you guys?" he asked.

"Put our initials all *over* these machines," Buddy said, "right, Charles?"

"You know it," Charles said.

Chapter 7

When Charles and Adam got back to the house, they found Mrs. Powell, reading the newspaper at the kitchen table while Mr. Powell fixed "a mess of franks and beans." Being, he said, as it was Saturday. After establishing that there was nothing he could do to help, Charles went with Adam to find Sarah and Jamie.

They were in the den, watching television, both wearing new outfits. Jamie's was significantly less conservative.

"New school clothes?" Charles guessed, sitting down on the couch next to Sarah.

Sarah made a face. "Pretty gross, hunh?"

"I'm sorry, Charles, I didn't hear you," Jamie said. "Did you say 'smashing and stylish'?"

"Snazzy," Charles said. "I said, snazzy."

"How come you're wearing 'em, anyway?" Adam asked. "I thought we were supposed to save stuff like that for school."

Sarah sighed. "Jamie has a theory."

Charles and Adam turned to hear it.

"Well." Jamie stretched dramatically. "It's very simple. If your clothes look all new and stiff, people think you made a big effort, right? But, if they look a little lived-in, *well*. . . ." She finished the sentence with a dramatic arm-span.

"That's because," Sarah said to Charles, "when we were in elementary school, she went to school the first day, and there was still a Health-Tex label hanging from her shirt, and she didn't notice it until everyone else did."

Jamie put down her Diet Pepsi. "You want me to tell him about the time your Toughskins ripped, and — "

"What are we watching, anyway?" Charles interrupted, sensing trouble.

"*Eight Is Enough*," Sarah said, obviously relieved to change the subject.

"Oh." Charles glanced around for the television section. "Is that all that's on?"

"We're *not* watching any stupid games," Jamie said. "*And* we're watching *Happy Days* next."

"Oh, come on," Charles said. "If we're going to watch reruns, *M*A*S*H* must be on at least *one* channel right now."

Sarah grabbed the remote control box and folded her hands around it so he couldn't get it.

"What about you?" he said to Adam. "You must have an opinion."

Adam shrugged. "I'll watch anything."

"Majority rules," Jamie said.

"Okay." Charles sighed. "Pass me a Pepsi, will you?"

After the kids were in bed that night, Charles sat at his desk going through the course registration book for what seemed like the seven-hundredth time. But registration was Monday, and he had to start making some decisions.

There was a knock on the door, and he put down the book.

"Come in," he said.

Mrs. Powell opened the door. "Am I interrupting anything?"

"No, not at all."

"Good." She leaned against the doorjamb. "I just came in to see how you're doing."

"Fine, thank you." Should he say ma'am? No, ma'am would sound stupid.

"You can call me Ellen or Mrs. Powell," she said. "Whichever makes you more comfortable."

"Probably Mrs. Powell," he said.

"Okay." She motioned toward the course book. "Figuring out what to take?"

"Well, *trying* to," he said.

"Have you declared a major yet?"

He shook his head. "We don't have to until the end of this year and — well, I'm still not sure."

"What do you like the best?"

He shook his head again. "I don't know. I mean, most of the stuff you take freshman year is so introductory — you know, Western Civ, English 101, Biology 101 — that it's really hard to tell. I think once I take some more advanced stuff, I'll have more of an idea."

She nodded. "That sounds sensible."

"The only thing I'm *sure* I'm not majoring in is economics."

"Pretty cutthroat?" she guessed.

"*Very* cutthroat," he said. "I think people are sort of more concerned about making money than they used to be."

Mrs. Powell laughed. "It certainly wasn't like that when *I* was in school."

"Were you there back in the sixties, when all the — " He stopped, flushing. "I'm sorry, I'm sorry, I'm not asking how old you are or anything."

She laughed again. "I was there during the end of it. It was funny because on the one hand, I was in antiwar demonstrations, but on the other, I was engaged to the children's father, who was at Annapolis."

"Was he antiwar, too?" Charles asked, before deciding that that was a pretty stupid question.

But Mrs. Powell was nodding. "In many ways, yes. But he had, as you may imagine, been raised to believe that when your country asked you to serve, you were supposed to do it, regardless. He also didn't think it would be fair to avoid serving because he had certain financial or educational advantages other people didn't have."

"Did he go over there? Vietnam, I mean?"

"On a hospital ship," she said. "And now, I think one of the main reasons he's stayed in the service is to try and help keep us *out* of conflicts."

Charles nodded. "Was your father-in-law in World War II and Korea and all?" he asked.

"Yes. He's a little more — old school — than my husband is."

Charles thought about that. "How did he feel about you being in antiwar things?"

Mrs. Powell smiled. "We've had a heated discussion or two over the years."

Charles smiled, too. No doubt.

"It must have been quite a surprise, coming home to find the Pembrokes leaving," she said.

That was an understatement.

"Although I guess that's an understatement," she added.

"Well" — he grinned sheepishly — "I was kind of surprised, yeah."

"I hope you didn't feel pressed into staying. I mean, I know things were pretty hectic here yesterday, and — well, we would certainly understand if you *didn't* want to stay on."

"No, I want to stay here," he said. "I mean, as long as you all are happy about it."

"Oh, I think it's going to work out *very* well," she said. "But I just wanted to be sure that you didn't have any second thoughts."

"No, ma'am. I mean, Mrs. Powell."

"Jill Pembroke gave me an overview of the guidelines all of you worked out, and I gather they were all right?"

Charles grinned. "The major one being no girls here overnight, or in any other — unseemly situation."

Mrs. Powell nodded. "That was right up there on the list, yes."

"Generally, I just gave them my class schedule, and they looked at their schedules, figured when I *needed* to be here, when they *hoped* I'd be here, and after that, it was up to me." He checked her expression. "Um, does that sound okay?"

"It sounds perfect," Mrs. Powell said.

Charles had agreed to meet Buddy outside of the gym at a quarter of ten for registration — so, naturally, Buddy didn't make it until quarter past.

"I know, I know," he said, untied sneakers flapping, eating a piece of jelly-smeared toast. "I got a late start."

Charles nodded, checking his watch. "I figured you would, so I didn't get here until five past."

"Oh." Buddy stopped chewing. "Well, *actually*, I was here at like, nine-thirty, but since you weren't — "

"Unh-hunh," Charles said.

"You don't believe me?"

"Unh-unh."

"Didn't think so." Buddy reached into the front pocket of his sweat shirt, taking out two more pieces of toast. "Want some? I've got plenty."

"Appetizing," Charles said, but he was hungry, and so took a piece anyway.

The gym was crowded with students; tables were set up representing each department, with English and economics having particularly long lines.

"Where you want to start?" Buddy asked.

Charles took out the file card he'd prepared with the list of his first, second, and alternate choices. "Don't you know what you're taking?"

"Well," Buddy put his sunglasses on top of his head — the better to scope the area — "I'm flexible."

"Right." Charles studied his list. "I think I'd better try for the foreign policy one — it'll probably close fast."

Buddy followed him toward the political science department's table. "If that's the one Cryden teaches, it's supposed to be *really* hard."

Charles nodded. "It's supposed to be good, though."

"*Two* twenty-page papers? Plus exams?" Buddy shook his head hard enough to knock his sunglasses down. He pushed them back up. "Won't catch *me* in there."

Charles pointed ahead of them in line at a tall, svelte blonde. "What if she's signing up for it?"

Buddy barely looked at her. "Twenty pages, Charles. Count 'em and weep." He looked at the girl more closely. "Besides, you could always introduce me."

"Don't hold your breath," Charles said.

"She might be signing up for Intro to American Government or something, anyway. I'll go find out." Buddy drifted up toward the front of the line to eavesdrop, then came back, frowning. "International Political Economy and Developing Nations, can you believe it?"

Charles grinned. "Out of your league?"

"Probably out of *Kissinger's* league." Buddy stood in line, tapping his foot, then he saw a very beautiful red-haired girl. "I'll see what *she's* taking." When he came back this time, he was smiling. "The Legislative Process. I can deal with that, right?"

Charles nodded. "Memorization, mostly."

"All *right*," Buddy said. "One down."

Neither course was closed, and Charles and Buddy each took their respective course cards, which they would present to their professors at the first class meeting, and which would be deposited in some computer somewhere.

"The world is increasingly automated," Buddy said, looking at his card. "Ever notice that?"

"Now and again," Charles said. "Where to now?"

"I was sort of thinking of taking Music Appreciation — you think that's stupid?"

"Clapping for Credit?" Charles said, using the nickname for the course.

"Yeah." Buddy sighed. "I guess it's not a very good idea."

"Let's go over to English," Charles suggested. "You're *bound* to find some pretty girls over there."

"Taking James Joyce, probably," Buddy said, but followed him over. "*You're* not signing up for that, are you?"

"Hey, I have limits, too," Charles said.

"Well, good." Buddy checked out the line, eating another piece of toast. "A lot of these girls are wearing black, Charles."

"Ten to one, it's worse over in the drama line."

"Hey, drama!" Buddy said. "We could take something fun over there!"

Charles laughed. "Do you *ever* not have fun, Buddy?"

"Hey, I'm taking the Legislative Process, right? *That* won't be fun. Besides," he said, "what's wrong with fun?"

"Nothing."

"Like in that movie *Arthur*," Buddy said. "When he was saying, 'Isn't fun the best thing to have?' I mean, you agree with that, right?"

Charles just laughed.

Only one of his first choice classes was closed, so Charles ended up with the foreign policy course, a Shakespeare course, Calculus and Differential Equations — which was probably a mistake, and Abnormal Psychology. Buddy, "for a goof," signed up for Abnormal Psychology, too. He also, after surveying the choices of a number of girls, registered for Twentieth Century American Fiction, and Marine Biology.

"*Marine* Biology?" Charles said, when he saw the course card.

Buddy smiled his more sincere smile. "I care deeply about these things, Charles."

"Right. Save it for your parents."

Buddy stopped smiling. "You think they'll buy it?"

"Probably not."

"You're probably right," Buddy said. "Oh, well, it's just, like, fish and stuff — it can't be too hard."

"You *hope*."

"Yeah. That girl was *seriously* pretty, though." He pulled over Charles's wrist to look at his watch. "Sid's. Pizza. Lunch."

"Sounds good to me," Charles said.

Chapter 8

It was the first day of school, and at least four sixths of the Powell household was pretty nervous. As a result, Mr. Powell's scrambled eggs, sausage, and biscuits weren't going over very well.

"Well, come on now," Mr. Powell said, clapping his hands. "Let's see some breakfast eating."

Charles helped himself politely to more eggs. "It's very good, sir."

"And what about you youngsters?" He pointed a spatula at them. "How do you expect to do well in school if you don't eat a good breakfast?"

"I *don't* expect to do well," Jamie said.

"Oh, come on, Jamie," Mrs. Powell said, fixing Sarah's hair. "For all you know, you're going to have some great teachers this year."

"Oh, yeah," Jamie said. "For sure."

Mr. Powell looked at her sternly. "A negative attitude won't help anything, young lady."

"Could I have another biscuit, please?" she asked, and he beamed, giving her two.

Charles looked down at his plate to hide his smile. Jamie was nobody's fool.

Satisfied with Sarah's hair, Mrs. Powell stepped back to examine her other two children. "Jamie, no mascara to school. Adam, I said to wear your *new* sweater."

Adam got up. "Can I wear the new commando one Grandpa gave me?"

"Do you mean, may you?" Mrs. Powell asked.

"May I?"

"No," she said. "You may not."

"How come you don't want me to take *my* mascara off?" Sarah wanted to know.

"Because you're such a dope you didn't put enough on," Jamie said.

Mrs. Powell bent down, squinting at Sarah's face. "She's right. But *don't* put on any more."

"Jamie says — "

Mrs. Powell cut her off. "Never mind what Jamie says."

"Although," Jamie said quietly, "what I said was *very* — "

"Whoa." Charles interrupted to prevent further trouble. "Am I the only one who's about to be late here?"

"Come on, troops," Mr. Powell said, his voice close to a bark. "You're supposed to be there at 0900 exactly. Let's move out. Double-time," he added, when the reaction wasn't fast enough to suit him.

"Hey, Mom!" Adam yelled from the safety of the stairs. "Do I have to wash off *my* mascara, too?"

Mrs. Powell sighed, finishing the last of her coffee. "Dad, because they're letting me come in late today, I probably won't be home until six or seven."

"No problem, no problem," Mr. Powell said and gestured toward Charles. "This young man and I can take care of dinner."

"Um, yes, sir," Charles said, resisting the urge to snap into a salute. He unzipped his knapsack, making sure he had his course cards, notebooks, pens, and anything else he might need. Like gum, to keep Buddy quiet during Abnormal Psychology. "Mrs. Powell, my last class ends at two, so I'll head back here then. You know, be here when the kids get home."

She nodded. "Thank you, Charles."

Sarah, back downstairs from brushing her teeth, looked at him wistfully. "I guess *you're* not nervous about school."

"Everyone's nervous the first day," he said. "*Teachers* are nervous."

Sarah nodded, but her expression was unconvinced.

"Don't worry," he said, "you'll be fine. It's a good school — the Pembrokes always really liked it."

She nodded again, still unconvinced. "So, you're coming home at two?"

"Well," Charles glanced at Mrs. Powell, "what I was thinking was, the school's pretty much on my way home, so I might swing by there and see if there's anyone who wants to walk the rest of the way with me."

Sarah's face relaxed. "You'd do that? I mean, you wouldn't be embarrassed or anything? Really?"

He grinned. "See you out front at two-fifteen."

Abnormal Psychology was his nine o'clock class and, surprisingly, Buddy was almost on time. He slipped into the seat Charles had saved for him, causing only a slight ruckus.

"Did I miss much?" he whispered.

"Just the syllabus and book list." Charles handed him copies of each.

"Thanks." Buddy took out a notebook, making enough noise for a few more people to turn around.

"Shhh," Charles said.

"Yeah, yeah, yeah, I know." Buddy was quiet for a minute. "Think this'll be like Psych 101? You know, read the book and see that you have, like, *everything*?"

"When did you read the book?" Charles asked out of the side of his mouth, trying to listen to the professor. "I never saw you."

"I bet it'll be like that," Buddy said, ignoring him. "Like, when you watch *St. Elsewhere* or something, and you have all the symptoms." He frowned. "I *hate* that."

"It's called hypochondria."

"See?" Buddy said. "*Another* thing I have."

"And there will be two hourly exams," the professor was saying, "as well as —"

"You know," Buddy said, "this might be a bad idea. Like, what if we have all the *abnormal* stuff?"

Charles sighed. "You can't drop the course on the *first* day."

"No, but —"

"And you know you're going to sleep through half the classes, anyway."

Buddy looked happier. "That's true."

"Boys?" the professor asked pleasantly.

"Sorry, ma'am," Buddy said. "The first day of class is always pretty exciting for me."

"Glad to hear it," she said, and went on.

"I invited these girls from my dorm to have lunch with us," Buddy said, after a few well-behaved minutes. "You mind?"

Charles shook his head, listening to the professor's explanation of how section meetings would be set up.

"They seem really nice," Buddy said. "I mean, they're only freshmen, but —"

"Shhh," Charles said.

"Oh. Sorry." Buddy sat back, folding his hands. Then he leaned forward. "Hey, you see that movie last night? The one where —"

Charles opened his knapsack. "Want some gum, Buddy?"

"Hey, wow, you have some?"

"Why would I ask you if I didn't?"

"Oh." Buddy thought about that. "That's true."

Charles handed him two pieces, taking one for himself.

"Thank you," Buddy said, and sat quietly chewing his gum for a minute. "Hey, did I ever tell you about the time —"

"*Shhh.*"

"Right," Buddy said. "Sorry." He sat back, looking around the room. "Lots of girls in here, Charles."

Charles nodded, writing down the building and room where his section group would be meeting.

"The way to meet them is, like, ask to see their notes and — hey, you're writing something down, did I miss it? Is it important?" Buddy pulled his notebook over, trying to see what he had written. "How do you know which one you're supposed to be in?"

"You *listen*," Charles said.

"Well, yeah, but — you think she'll tell me?" He indicated the professor. "If I go up to her after class?"

"I think she'll *slap* you if you go up to her after class."

"Oh." Buddy looked worried. "You think I'm already on her bad side? Should I drop the course?"

"You should shut up," Charles said. "Take some notes."

"Oh. Okay."

"Thank you."

Buddy sat without fidgeting for almost two minutes. "Just one thing," he whispered.

"What," Charles said.

Buddy grinned. "Can I borrow a pen?"

The rest of the day was relatively uneventful. He had lunch with Buddy and the two girls — who were very nice and very immature. He went to his first foreign policy class, which was going to be both as hard and as good as he had heard. He went to the bookstore and spent an outrageously high sum of money on his new books.

At two-fourteen, he was in front of the junior high school, waiting for Sarah. When they'd left for school, Jamie hadn't decided if she wanted to walk home with them — it might cramp her style, she said — and Adam's school got out half an hour later than the girls' school did.

At two-fifteen exactly, Sarah came out in a crush of escaping students, looking around, nervously smiling when she saw him.

"So, how was it?" he asked, taking her books.

She made a face.

"Jamie going to join us?"

Sarah shook her head. "She already has about *nine* best friends."

"Did you meet anyone you liked?"

She shook her head.

"Well, the first day's always hard," he said. "Are your teachers nice?"

She nodded.

"Well, *that's* good."

She nodded.

"What are you trying to do," he said, "talk my ear off?"

She smiled a little.

"I guess this is one of those times I should have a Life Saver available," he said.

She managed a little bigger smile.

"There's an ice-cream store on the way home — how about a milk shake?"

She nodded.

Jamie came walking out of the school with two boys and three girls. She saw them and ran over.

"I'm going to go to McDonald's with them, okay, Charles?" she said. "If I'm back by three-thirty or four?"

"At the *very* latest," he said. "And don't spoil your dinner."

She laughed. "You're worse than my *grandfather*, even." She jogged back toward her new friends. "See you later."

"See?" Sarah said, sounding very unhappy. "She has a million friends already."

"Well, I'm sure she — "

Jamie came jogging back. "Hey, Sarah, you want to come with us?"

Sarah hesitated.

"Why don't you?" Charles said. "You'll have fun."

"No, I — " Sarah hesitated. "They're all older, and — "

"That doesn't matter," Jamie said, her voice only a little impatient. "Just come on, okay?"

"No, I —" Sarah looked at Charles for help.

"Well, maybe it's been kind of a tough day," he said. "How about she comes next time?"

Jamie shrugged. "Okay, whatever. See you guys later."

As she left, Charles looked down at Sarah. "You might have had a pretty good time."

"But I don't *know* them," Sarah said. "And — I can never think of anything to say."

"Well" — he put a comforting hand on her shoulder — "slow and steady wins the race, right?"

"I'm just *slow*."

"Well, so long as you *finish* the race," he said.

"Is that supposed to be profound?"

He nodded. "It's *very* profound. Write it down."

They were walking across the parking lot when Sarah stopped, turning in the other direction.

Charles stopped, too. "Did I miss something?"

"They're from my *class*," she said, and he saw two girls walking along in their direction.

"So, say hello. While I'm here to back you up."

She shook her head. "I can't — I don't *know* them."

"It's not that hard," he said. "All you have to do is —"

"I know, I've done it," she said. "I just *hate* it."

"Okay, but this is a perfect — "

The two girls stopped.

"Hi," one of them said. "Aren't you in our class?"

"I — " Sarah's voice squeaked a little, so she just nodded.

"I'm Lori," the girl said. "And that's Andrea."

"H-hi," Sarah managed. "I'm Sarah."

Andrea looked shyly at Charles. "Are you her brother?"

"No," Sarah said, "he — well, he lives with us."

The girls looked impressed.

"Do you pick her up every day?" Lori asked.

"Now and again," Charles said, smiling at them, and the two girls giggled shyly.

"Well, see you tomorrow," Andrea said to Sarah.

Sarah nodded. "Yeah, s-see you tomorrow."

"Well, *that* wasn't so hard," Charles said, when the girls were out of earshot.

"No," Sarah said, sounding surprised. "It wasn't." She looked up at him. "*Can* you pick me up every day?"

He laughed. "We'll see."

Chapter 9

With school underway life fell into a more normal pattern, and Charles found himself missing the Pembrokes, but getting used to — and enjoying — living with the Powells. His courses were as demanding as he had expected — the calculus class was downright *impossible* — and he was having to spend a lot more time studying than he had freshman year. Buddy, of course, felt that skimming a chapter every week or so was more than enough effort to put out.

It was Tuesday, and when Charles got home, Adam was sitting in the kitchen, wearing a baseball cap and glove, holding a ball in his free hand.

"Hi," Charles said, checking the mail on the table. A letter from his parents and a postcard from the Pembrokes with a picture of the Kingdome on it. "Waiting for a bus?"

"No," Adam said uncertainly. "I was kind of — you know, if you weren't busy — that is — "

Charles read the postcard, which was more enthusiastic than informative, signed by all three of the Pembroke kids. "I bet you want to play a little catch," he said.

"If *you* want to," Adam said.

Charles went over to the refrigerator to get a glass of orange juice. "Yeah, sure. Where're your sisters?"

"Sarah's reading and Jamie's at ballet."

"Are we supposed to pick her up?"

Adam nodded. "At four-thirty."

"Okay." Charles drained his glass, then put it in the dishwasher. "I'll go say hello to Sarah and get my glove."

Sarah was lying on the couch in the living room, her face obscured by a book. She was *usually* in that position.

"Hi, Sarah," Charles said cheerfully. "Read any good books lately?"

" 'How do I love thee? Let me count the ways,' " she said without looking up.

Elizabeth Barrett Browning. " 'I think that I shall never see,' " Charles said, " 'A poem lovely as a tree.' "

"Joyce Kilmer," Sarah said, still not looking up.

"Okay." Charles thought for a minute. " 'The year's at the spring, and day's at the morn.' "

"Robert Browning," she said. "Ask a *hard* one."

"Okay." He wasted a certain amount of time every couple of days looking these things up to try and stump her. But he was actually starting to appreciate poetry more. " 'I sing of brooks, of blossoms, birds and bowers, of April, May, of June and July-flowers.' "

She bit her lip, and he knew he had her. "Robert Frost?" she guessed.

"Robert *Herrick*," he said. "Back in the seventeenth century."

"Oh." She closed her eyes, trying to remember. "You mean, 'Gather ye rosebuds while ye may'?"

Charles nodded. "That's the one."

"So, I got two out of three."

"Two and a half," he said. "You *did* know who he was." He continued toward his room. "We're going to play catch — you want to, too?"

"No, thanks."

"You want to come when we go pick up Jamie?"

She lowered the book. "Can we go see Grandpa at the store?"

"Sure." In his room, he took his baseball glove down from the closet shelf, automatically punching the pocket a few times. There had been a period in his life — when he was twelve until he was about fourteen — when it had been his prized possession, and he had spent hours with neat's-foot oil and saddle soap, conditioning it and breaking it in. His father was a big Pirates' fan, and they had gone to a lot of games, Charles always bringing his trusty glove along, just in case. The closest he had ever come to catching a ball was three rows, but his recurring fantasy had been that he would make a spectacular catch in the stands, the manager would leap out of the dugout and shout, "Sign that kid up!" A fantasy shared, he suspected, by most of the free world.

"Come on, Charles, let's go!" Adam called from the front door.

"Right!" Charles called back. "I'm just going to put some sweat pants on."

The baseball glove had stopped being his prized possession when he was fourteen and decided, courtesy of the Steelers, that he wanted to be a wide receiver, and he and his friends spent hours trying to throw, and catch, perfect spirals. Then, by the time he was sixteen, he was growing tall instead of broad, and his new favorite possession was a basketball. Now that he had stopped growing, period, he was probably most fond of his running shoes.

Adam was suddenly in the doorway. "What's taking you so long?"

"I was — ruminating," Charles said.

"What's that?"

"It's a good word," Charles said. "Look it up."

Adam leaned into the living room. "Sarah, what's 'ruminate' mean?"

"It means 'think,' " she said, reading.

"Reflect upon," Charles added. He put on his old Pirates' hat and headed for the door. "Let's go."

For the first few minutes, they threw the ball back and forth easily.

"I have trouble throwing the ball hard," Adam said.

"You should never throw the ball hard until you're warmed up," Charles said immediately.

"I mean, even *after* that. I mean — in general."

"Well, let me watch what you're doing." Charles paid careful attention as Adam threw the ball to him this time, and saw the problem right away. "You're stepping with the wrong leg, Adam."

Adam looked down. "What do you mean?"

"Well, you're right-handed, right? And you're striding with the right leg."

Adam was still looking down. "Yeah, so?"

"It throws you off balance." Charles came over to demonstrate. "See, you want to step with the *opposite* leg. Like — like you're serving a tennis ball, okay? See, your right arm is back, most of your weight's on your right leg, you bring the ball forward," he demonstrated, "and your weight changes to your left leg, see? You get a lot more power *and* balance."

"Oh." Adam tried it. "Oh, I get it."

"The other way you're just throwing with your arm. This way, you get your whole body behind it." Charles trotted back over to where he had been. "Give it a try for real."

Adam threw the ball a little wild, but a

lot harder. "My *body* still wants to do it the other way."

"It'll take you a while to get used to it, that's all." Charles grinned. "And it'll definitely cut down on those rotator cuff injuries."

Adam laughed, catching the ball and throwing it back. Correctly. "Can you teach me how to throw a knuckleball, too?"

"Well, I know the *principle*," Charles said. "But I can't really do it."

"Can you show me?"

Charles shrugged, motioning him over. "See," he demonstrated, "you don't actually use your knuckles, you use your fingertips. Your hand's probably not big enough to do it with three, so just use all of your fingers. Then," he drew his arm back to show him, "the point is to let it go so there's no spin or anything on it. That way, if there's any wind or, I don't know, humidity even, the ball bounces around all over the place. And you don't throw it hard, because you want to give the wind a chance to work on it. If you throw it hard, the ball just goes in there flat and — " He made a whistling sound to indicate a home run.

"You know a lot," Adam said, impressed.

"My *father* knows a lot," Charles said. "And I had a couple of pretty good coaches."

"*My* last coach was kind of mean," Adam said.

"I had a couple of those, too," Charles

agreed. He flipped Adam the ball. "Why would you want to throw a knuckleball, anyway? That's for people whose arms are thrown out."

Adam shrugged. "I don't know. I thought it'd be fun."

Charles nodded. "Yeah, I used to fool around with it, too, but my Little League coach said — " He stopped. "Do you really want to hear all this junk?"

"Yeah!" Adam said.

"Okay, this is today's last fun fact." Charles took his glove off, felt too much like a coach himself, and put it back on. "He always used to say" — he looked solemn — "'Just put the pellet over the plate, son. Nothing fancy. Just throw a hard one and a change.'" He went on, anticipating Adam's, "What if I don't *have* a change-up?" "'And if you don't have a change, throw a hard one, and a *really* hard one.'"

Adam looked confused. "I can't even try a *curve*?"

"I think his point was, as long as you had control, that was all you really needed, and once your arm stopped growing, you could experiment a little." He tossed Adam the ball. "Enough fun facts, already. Let's just play for a while."

"Will you teach me more next time?" Adam asked eagerly.

"Sure thing," Charles promised.

They threw the ball around for a while; Adam's energy and enthusiasm unflagging;

Charles keeping an eye on his watch so they wouldn't be late to pick up Jamie.

"We'd better head along," he said at four-fifteen.

Adam looked disappointed. "Do we have to?"

"Yeah, we don't want to be late." He handed Adam his glove. "Here, do me a favor and go get Sarah, and I'll start the car."

When they got to the ballet school, Jamie was out in front, very chic in her pink sweat shirt, warm-up skirt, and leg warmers.

"How was your lesson?" Charles asked as she got into the car.

"Okay." Jamie dumped her knapsack on the floor in the backseat. "Can I sit up front?"

"No," Adam said, tightening his seat belt to indicate he wasn't going anywhere.

"Can we go to the mall and look around?" she asked.

"We're going to go see Grandpa," Sarah said, also in the back.

"Oooh." Jamie reached up to fix her hair, taking it out of its bun. "All *kinds* of guys hang out there."

"*That* I'd like to see," Sarah said. "You, picking up boys, in front of Grandpa."

"That's true." Jamie put her hair back up in the bun.

There were only a few customers in the surplus store, and as they went in, they could hear Mr. Powell talking.

"Nothing like it for building character," he was saying to a boy buying a pair of Army slacks and two webbed belts. "Never met a man yet who didn't — " He stopped, seeing them. "Look, here're my grandchildren!"

"We ran out of ammunition," Adam said cheerfully. "So Charles drove us over right away."

The boy buying the pants and belts backed up a couple of steps.

"My grandson thinks he has a sense of humor," Mr. Powell explained to him.

"Yeah, really." Jamie pushed Adam off balance. "When have we *ever* run out of ammunition?"

"Uh, see you later," the boy said, taking his change and his bag and hurrying out.

Mr. Powell came around the counter. "What brings you all over here?"

"Charles!" Adam said, and laughed at his own joke.

"We just came to say hello, sir," Charles said. "And see if you wanted a ride home."

Mr. Powell shook his head. "Think I'll walk it, soldier. Get my exercise in." He turned to his grandchildren. "So. Who wants a souvenir?"

"Are we allowed?" Sarah asked hesitantly.

"Sure," he said. "Not a man who works here doesn't have grandchildren. Why Francis over there," he pointed at a man with white hair helping someone near the back of the store, "he has *eight*."

"One more on the way," Francis said.

"There you go," Mr. Powell said. "Now, what would you all like?"

As Mr. Powell was looking for souvenirs, Charles wandered around the store. Neatly folded stacks of Army and work pants, of long underwear and flannel shirts. Camouflage T-shirts. Uniform shirts. Bomber jackets. Various caps and helmets and even berets. Almost everything was navy blue or olive green.

"Look, Charles." Sarah came over with a small, leather-bound field diary. "For me to write in."

"That's really nice," he said.

"Let's go see what Adam and Jamie get."

They walked back to the front of the store, where Jamie had selected a watch cap, which she adjusted to a very sporty tilt, and Adam had decided on a steel mess kit.

"What about Charles?" Adam asked.

Charles flushed, feeling a little like Dorothy in *The Wizard of Oz*. "Oh, I really don't — "

"No, the boy's right," Mr. Powell said. "You should have something, too." He studied him for a minute, both arms folded thoughtfully across his chest.

"I really don't — " Charles started.

Mr. Powell snapped his fingers. "A canteen! You can use it as a water bottle when you and that Buddy character play basketball." He fished around inside a display case, coming out with a canteen with a green canvas cover. "There you go. First-rate."

Charles took it, feeling very touched —

and feeling more and more like a member of this family. "Thank you, sir."

"Hey, that's really nice," Adam said. "Do you like it?"

"Yeah," Charles said, and grinned. "I like it a lot."

Chapter 10

At lunch the next day, Charles came out of the cafeteria line, holding his tray, looking around for Buddy. He saw him at their usual table — by the window, with an excellent view of the door — and carried his tray over there.

He put his tray down on the table. "Hey, Buddy, what's up?"

"I don't know," Buddy said. "Nothing much."

"You didn't invite any lunch companions?"

"Hunh?" Buddy shook his head. "I mean, no."

"What, are you slipping? I mean —" Charles noticed that the food on Buddy's tray was untouched. "What's wrong?"

"I don't know." Buddy shook his head again. "I should have seen it coming, but — something terrible's happened."

"What?" Charles asked, alarmed now. "Is everything okay with your family?"

"No, no, it's nothing like that. It's just — "
Buddy let out an unhappy breath, slouching forward onto his arms. "I *like* one of my classes, Charles."

Charles stared at him. "You're putting me on."

"No, I'm not. One minute, I'm the same old happy-go-lucky — "

"*That's* what you're so upset about?"

"Well, yeah," Buddy said. "I mean — yeah."

"I don't believe you, Buddy." Charles reached for the salt and pepper. "From the way you looked, I thought — I don't know what I thought, but it wasn't good."

"It *is* terrible," Buddy said. "I mean, you don't understand at all. I *really* like it. I pay attention to the lectures, I take notes — I got an A on the first research thing, even."

"But that's *good* news, Buddy." Charles opened a couple of little ketchup packets for his french fries. "I don't get why you're so upset."

"You know what my parents will say?"

"Thank God?" Charles guessed.

"Exactly," Buddy said. "They'll think — I've found my niche. That I'll always get good grades and behave responsibly and — "

"Oh, come on, Buddy. They know you better than that."

"That's what *you* think," Buddy said. "When my brother got his first A in college, they practically — "

"So, wait," Charles interrupted. "Which

class is it, anyway? I mean, I *know* it's not Abnormal Psychology."

"Marine Biology," Buddy said, actually looking enthusiastic. "Like, I only took it because that girl Peggy was signing up —"

"The one it turned out is practically engaged to Burt Kravitz?"

Buddy nodded. "Yeah. So, I figured the whole course was going to be a total loss, but it's really good. I mean, it's really interesting. There's all this stuff about evolution and ecosystems and the balance of —"

"You'd better watch it, Buddy," Charles said, grinning. "You're going to turn into a brain."

Buddy's nod was glum. "I know. I mean, *nineteen* years of making a totally cool reputation, and *now*, in just a few weeks —" He made a throwing motion with his arm. "Out the window."

Charles laughed. "You know what's funny about it?"

"Nothing."

"The fact that I *know* you're serious. I mean, you probably *are* upset about it."

"I *am*," Buddy said. "And you know what happened today? My professor was going around the class, asking for comments about" — he grinned a little — "well, fish stuff, to the lay person — and when he got to me, he said, 'Well, Mr. Lembeck, I'm sure you have something intelligent to contribute,' and" — he paused significantly — "*no one laughed.*"

"*Did* you have something intelligent to contribute?" Charles asked.

"Well, yeah," Buddy said. "Actually."

Charles laughed.

"So, what do you think? Should I drop the class?"

Charles laughed again. "No, you shouldn't drop the class. You should be glad — people *come* to college to find out what they like."

"I just came to meet girls."

"So, think of this as a fringe benefit," Charles said.

"Oh." Buddy considered that. "Yeah, that makes sense." Looking happier, he picked up one of his hamburgers, taking a bite. "Just promise me you'll slap me or something, if I start getting — I don't know — smart."

"Count on it." Charles picked up his own hamburger, very amused. "If it cheers you up, I *hate* one of my classes this semester."

"Calculus, right?"

"Well — yeah," Charles said.

"What, and that *surprises* you?"

"Well — yeah," Charles said. "I mean, I figured it'd be really hard and all, but I was pretty good at math in high school, and — I even liked it. But — I got a C-minus on the first test. *And* I hate it."

"Well — it'll be better when they put it on the curve, right?"

"That *is* after the curve," Charles said.

"Oh," Buddy said. "So, what are you going to do — drop it?"

"No. The deadline for deciding to take

something Pass/Fail is Friday, and — "

Charles sighed. "I don't know. I mean, I don't have a major yet, but I always figured — I mean, somewhere in the back of my head — I mean, I used to *like* science and math. People always figured I'd end up in med school, even."

"A teacher," Buddy said. "Ten to one, you end up being a teacher."

Charles groaned. "Oh, no."

"*Junior high.*"

"No way."

"*And,*" Buddy paused for effect, "a coach."

Which sounded more than plausible. Charles sighed. Ask not for whom the bell tolls, it tolls for — "And what are you going to be doing?" he asked. "Swimming around, looking at coral?"

Buddy laughed. "With *my* luck, I'll end up working in a bait shop."

They both laughed. Uneasily.

"Let's go find some more food," Buddy suggested.

"Let's go find some *lunch* companions," Charles said.

Any kind of serious talk about careers was always pretty sobering, so Charles went out of his way to make sure he had fun the rest of the day. Especially since he knew he had *a lot* of studying to do that night. He hung around after his last class to play basketball with Buddy and some other guys they knew; then, when he got home, he played a game of chess with Sarah *and* a game of Stratego with Adam. And then, after dinner, when Adam suggested that ice cream would be a swell idea, Charles agreed to take all three of them — on the condition that *they* do the dishes.

"*I'm* sitting in the front this time," Jamie said, as they went out to the car.

"I call it on the way home!" Sarah said.

"I call it next time!" Adam said.

Charles opened the driver's door. "Don't fight about it, or I'll make *all* of you sit in the back."

"They started it," Adam said.

"Jamie started it," Sarah said.

"No way!" Jamie protested. "Adam started it *before* when he — "

Charles turned on the engine. "Last call for ice cream."

They all jumped into the car.

There were a lot of people at Baskin-Robbins, and they had to wait in line.

"How big a thing can we get?" Adam asked.

Charles checked his wallet. "Your mother gave me ten dollars — and I think she wants a little change."

"Okay," Adam said, looking at the price list. "So *I'll* get a super-large banana split, and you guys can get small cones."

"Hey, that's not fair!" Sarah said. "I wanted a — "

"Let's all get double cones," Charles suggested. "Period."

"Do you think I'll get fat?" Jamie asked, touching her stomach. "I mean, eating ice cream just this once?"

"You *always* eat ice cream," Sarah said.

"Yeah, really," Adam agreed. "Practically every time I come in the kitchen, you're eating ice cream."

Sarah nodded. "Except when she's eating cookies."

"Besides," Adam said, "she's *already* fat."

Jamie put her hands on her hips. "Are you going to let them do that, Charles?"

Charles pretended he hadn't been listening. "I'm sorry, what? Were you all talking about something?"

"I *know* you heard them," Jamie said.

"Heard what?"

"Forget it," Jamie said, reading the list of ice-cream flavors.

"Next," a harried-looking boy said when it was finally their turn.

"Oh, hi," Charles said. "We'll have four double cones. One — " he tried to remember what all of them had told him — "mocha chip and mint chocolate chip, one pralines and cream with rocky road, one chocolate chocolate chip and — what was the other one, Adam?"

"Pumpkin," he said.

"Pumpkin." Charles shook his head. "Okay. A scoop of pumpkin with the chocolate chocolate chip, and one — " He realized that he hadn't decided what he wanted. "One, uh — well." He scanned the list of flavors, aware that the people behind him were growing quite impatient. To say nothing of the guy waiting on them. "Uh, butter pecan. Butter pecan and fudge whirl."

The boy nodded, and started scooping.

Sarah pulled on Charles's sleeve. "Is it too late to change mine?"

He looked at the boy. "Is it too late to change hers?"

"Which one *is* hers?" the boy asked.

"I can't remember." He looked at Sarah. "Which one was yours?"

"The mocha and mint chip," she said. "Can I have black raspberry instead of the mocha chip?"

Charles looked at the boy, who scraped the mocha chip off the cone and started over.

"Charles, can you ask him if I can have a cake cone?" Adam asked.

Cake cone. Charles frowned. "What's a cake cone?"

"He means waffle cone," Sarah said. "The ones that taste like Styrofoam."

"Oh." Charles looked at the boy. "Is it too late to put the pumpkin and the chocolate chip on a waffle cone?"

The boy stopped scooping chocolate chocolate chip and exchanged the sugar cone for a waffle cone. Finished, he handed each of the cones up to Charles. "You guys all set?"

"You guys all set?" Charles asked.

Sarah looked hesitant. "Could we get something to drink, too?"

"Sure," Charles said. "Could we have three small Cokes?"

The boy turned to get them.

"Charles — " Jamie started.

"Right," he said. "Could we have *two* small Cokes, and a Diet Coke?"

"Right," the boy said.

He brought over the three drinks, then paused. "You *sure* everyone's all set here?"

Charles nodded. "I'm sure."

The boy rang up the sale. "That'll be eight dollars and forty-five cents."

Charles handed him the money, feeling guilty for having been so much trouble. "Uh, keep the change."

The boy grinned. "Thanks." He looked down the counter. "Who's next?" he asked.

It was later, and his foreign policy paper was going *nowhere*. The paper wasn't due for a couple of days — but, still. He hated doing work at the last minute.

A snack. Maybe what he needed was a snack.

He pushed away from his desk, going out to the darkened living room toward the kitchen. Pushing the door open, he stopped in the middle of his yawn, seeing Mrs. Powell sitting at the kitchen table with a cup of coffee.

"Oh, hi." Automatically, he looked down to see what he was wearing. T-shirt and sweat pants. Good. "I'm sorry, I didn't — excuse me. I should have knocked."

Mrs. Powell waved that aside with one hand. "Trouble sleeping?"

"Trouble *studying*." He shook the kettle to see how much water was in it, then added a little more. "Isn't cocoa supposed to be the drink of choice this late?"

"Well, they say chocolate keeps you awake, too, so I'd just as soon have coffee." She picked up the mug, sipping some. "There are plenty of cookies in the jar, if you want some."

"Yeah, that sounds good." He opened the jar, taking out several. "Would you like some, too?"

"Oh — maybe one." Mrs. Powell folded the letter she had been reading and put it in an envelope, Charles recognizing Commander Powell's handwriting.

"I guess you must miss him a lot," he said, sitting down.

She nodded. "I knew what I was getting into, though. Mostly, I just pray that he can spend his career on *peacetime* maneuvers."

Charles nodded, too.

"He'll have to get shore leave *sometime* soon. Or get transferred back."

"Jamie was telling me he's pretty sure he'll be stationed near here?"

"Washington, at the very least," Mrs. Powell agreed. "He has a few more years yet before he can think about retiring and getting into civilian life."

"Which he'll probably do?"

"Oh, I think so," Mrs. Powell said. "He's

not nearly as — regimented — as his father is."

The water was boiling, and Charles got up to fix himself a cup of instant cocoa. "What *is* he like?"

"Well, out of the children, I'd say Jamie is the most like him."

Charles tried, unsuccessfully, to picture a military Jamie.

"He has a certain — 'brash' isn't quite the word — no, I guess it's more of an aggressive joie de vivre," she decided.

That, he could picture. "I'm sure he's very nice," Charles said. "I'm looking forward to meeting him."

Mrs. Powell nodded. "He's thoughtful, like Sarah. Energetic, like Adam." She smiled. "*Punctual,* like his father." She took another cookie from the plate Charles had put on the table. "We both just thought it was time to give the children a chance to put down a few roots."

"And you want to stay at your job," Charles guessed.

"Well — more or less," she said wryly.

"You don't like it?"

"I like *working,*" Mrs. Powell said. "At this point, I really couldn't do without that. But this *particular* job — well, it's a lot more grunt work and a lot less management than I'd expected."

Charles took a cookie himself. "You could get another job."

"To be honest with you," she said, "I felt

lucky to get *this* one. I mean, bad enough to have been away from the work force for quite some time, on *top* of the fact that I'm married to someone who can be transferred pretty indiscriminately."

"So, I guess you'll stay with this job."

She nodded. "That's a pretty safe bet." She started to take a cookie, changed her mind, and drank some coffee instead. "How about you? Are *you* happy with your job?"

"Actually," Charles said, "I kind of think of school as my job. I mean, I like it here."

"I certainly don't know what we'd do without you. The children, especially."

"Well —" don't say shucks, he ordered himself — "thank you. I'm getting pretty fond of them, too."

They sat without talking for a minute, but it was a pleasant silence. Then Mrs. Powell glanced at the clock.

"Oh, no, will you look at that?" she said.

Charles looked. Quarter past two.

"I don't know about *you*," Mrs. Powell said, "but I'm going to have a little trouble getting up in the morning."

His first class was at nine. And he *still* had a lot of studying left. "I think that makes two of us," Charles said.

Chapter 11

He *was* pretty tired the next day, but since
he'd started college he was generally pretty
tired. He got to campus just in time to make
his nine o'clock psychology class, and as he
went into the small auditorium where it was
held, he was surprised to see Buddy already
there.

Charles sat down, dropping his knapsack
on the floor. "What are *you* doing here?"

Buddy shrugged. "Dining hall ran out of
danishes."

"So you didn't have anything better to do."

Buddy nodded. "More or less, yeah. Did
you finish your paper?"

"More or less." Charles took out his notebook, turning to the page where he'd left off
the class before and dating it.

Buddy shook his head, watching him. "No
wonder everyone's always borrowing your
notes."

"Are you going to let me listen today, or
are you going to talk?"

"Oh, come on," Buddy said. "Dr. Feinberg wouldn't be able to concentrate if I *didn't* talk. I think it'd throw her off."

"Well, she must be *used* to it by now, anyway."

As class started, Charles took careful notes to make up for the fact that he was a little behind in the reading. Buddy seemed to be taking notes, too, and Charles glanced over to see what he was doing. There was a list of key words like "deviance" and "psychosis" on the left side of the page, and on the right side, Buddy was drawing stick figures who were wearing sunglasses, skiing, and surfing. He saw Charles looking and drew a quick, stiff stick figure with a bow tie, scrawling "Charles" underneath.

"Right," Charles said, and focused on the blackboard, where their professor was putting up a list of statistics. When he glanced back at the picture, Buddy had given "Charles" a briefcase, a flat-top haircut, and *very* prominent ears. Also, Pee Wee Herman dancing shoes, with three-inch heels. The addition of short, baggy bellbottoms was *too* insulting, and Charles turned to an empty page in his own notebook.

He drew a picture of a fat boy with too many teeth and lots of wild curly hair. He gave the boy a cut-off T-shirt, stomach protruding, and split-to-the-seams drawstring bathing trunks. And flip-flops. Ugly flip-flops. He drew the boy a bucket of chicken to hold in one hand, and a half-eaten drumstick with flies gathering around it in the other. Then, he wrote "Buddy" at the bottom.

"This is *war*," Buddy said, and flipped to a fresh page. He started with the face, giving "Charles" six strands of hair, buck teeth, a bulbous nose, one regular ear, and one badly deformed ear. Next to the deformed ear, he wrote "cauliflower ear," and Charles had to laugh. Sensing the professor frowning in their direction, he quickly put on a more sober expression. An alert, intelligent expression.

Oblivious to all of this, Buddy kept drawing. "Charles" had a skinny neck with a large Adam's apple, and was wearing a muscle T-shirt that revealed nothing more than puny arms, a sunken chest, and a tiny but definite potbelly. Next to the potbelly, he wrote "love handles," and Charles laughed again.

Next, Buddy drew "Charles" what looked like a little skirt, writing "culottes" next to it. He drew little stick legs with knobby knees and white athletic socks. Charles wasn't quite sure what the shoes were supposed to be, but Buddy wrote "Dr. Scholl's" next to them. Then, he put an oversized watch on one wrist and let that hand hold a copy of the magazine *Tiger Beat*. In the other hand, he let "Charles" hold something, which he labeled "Bermuda bag." As a final touch, he gave the figure a pair of glasses, and wrote at the bottom of the picture, "Charles Goes to the Beach." He handed the picture to Charles to study more carefully, and they both laughed, loudly enough for people near them to turn around.

Their professor paused significantly in her lecture, and they put on solemn, studious expressions.

"Top *that*," Buddy whispered when she had turned back to the board.

Charles gave his picture a completely bald head, except for one curly hair sticking straight up. He drew jughandle ears, each with an assortment of wild-looking earrings. On the face, he let the eyebrows meet together in the middle, the eyes so close-set that they seemed to meet, too. Instead of buck teeth, he let a fang hang out of the smiling mouth, and gave "Buddy" no neck at all. He drew him a leisure suit, with the collar points spread out over the lapels and the cuffs too short, writing "lime green" next to it. There was a wide gap of fatness between the shirt and pants, and he drew a big key ring to hang from the belt on a chain. He gave "Buddy" round-toed sneakers with smile-faces drawn on them, no socks, and hairy ankles. The dying bouquet in his right hand didn't look right, so Charles wrote "milkweed" next to it to be sure that was clear. In the other hand he put a record album, which he wrote "Bee-Gees" on. Then, under the picture, he wrote "Buddy Goes to His First Dance." He passed the notebook over to Buddy, and they both broke up completely.

Their professor stopped her lecture. "Would it be too much trouble," she asked, "to explain what you two find so amusing?"

They looked at each other, and laughed even harder.

"Perhaps you'd feel better if you left the auditorium for a few minutes to get control of yourselves," she suggested.

"Are we getting thrown out of class?" Buddy said, laughing.

Charles stopped laughing. "Looks that way, yeah."

"Can they *do* that in college?"

"Looks that way, yeah."

Dr. Feinberg cleared her throat.

"Uh, right." Charles stood up. "Excuse us."

Buddy just laughed, getting his books together. "Don't forget your purse," he said to Charles.

"Feel free to return," Dr. Feinberg said. "If you're able."

Trying to get out of the row, Charles dropped half of his books, and Buddy almost fell down laughing.

"Those darn heels," Buddy said to Charles, laughing even harder. "Excuse us," he said to Dr. Feinberg.

They stumbled out of the auditorium, practically falling onto the floor in the hall.

"So what do you think?" Buddy said, holding his stomach. "We going to make dean's list?"

Charles looked worried at first, then he glanced at Buddy and started to laugh. "Can't miss," he said.

That night, after being assured that there would be plenty of Entenmann's cake and other such health foods around, Buddy came over to the Powells' house to study. "It'll be great, Charles," he'd said. "We'll set a good example for the kids." "Like the example we set in psychology today?" Charles had asked. And Buddy had laughed again. "*Just* like that," he said.

Actually, although he knew he should probably be more concerned — or feel *guilty*, at least — Charles spent most of the *day* laughing. It was the culottes, he decided, that had really set him off. Buddy thought the milkweed had been a nice touch.

"You're certainly in a good mood tonight," Mrs. Powell remarked, coming through the living room as they were making a mild effort to study.

"Just that kind of day, ma'am," Buddy said.

"Do either of you know if anyone *else* under this roof is doing homework?"

Charles nodded. "I'm pretty sure Sarah is."

Mrs. Powell grinned wryly. "Safe bet." She continued upstairs. "If you see Jamie before I do, can you remind her that her father's going to be calling at nine, and she should stay off the phone?"

"Sure thing, Mrs. Powell," Charles said. Jamie had, indeed, already made about nine best friends, and they all spent a lot of time on the phone.

"So, what do you think," Buddy said as Charles proofread his foreign policy paper. "Is Dr. Feinberg going to yell at us next time, or just pretend it didn't happen?"

Charles checked the dictionary to make sure he had spelled "prescient" correctly. Yes. Good. "She'll say something arch and leave it at that," he said, closing the dictionary.

"Remember in high school? When they could put all those comments after your name?"

Charles changed one of his commas to a semicolon to emphasize the next clause a little more. "Our school was on a computer — we got little numbers, and you had to look them up on the side."

"I bet you got a lot of 'Outstanding Student' and 'Always Prepared' remarks," Buddy guessed.

Charles nodded. " 'Joy to be around,' 'May marry my only daughter' — all that stuff."

"*We* got comments," Buddy said. "I always got like 'Does not work to potential' and 'Talks to his neighbors.' "

Charles laughed. "They had *your* number, hunh?"

"My chemistry teacher even put that I was 'unruly.' "

Charles looked up from his paper. "That exact word?"

Buddy nodded.

"I guess it's better than 'boisterous.'"

Buddy nodded again. "Or 'Seems to need therapy.'" He grinned. "Wonder what Dr. Feinberg'd put?"

Charles darkened a hyphen that was too light. "'Immature cretins.'"

"*Cretins*?" Buddy said. "I think she'd stick with 'Boys will be boys.'"

Charles laughed. "Right."

Jamie came wandering down the stairs, carrying an armload of laundry.

"Jamie," Charles started, "your mother says —"

She nodded. "Not to talk on the phone, I know."

"Oh. Okay." He went back to his paper, inverting two letters.

"Going to Goodwill?" Buddy asked, indicating her laundry — all bright, flashy clothes.

"Ha," she said. "Charles, I'm doing permanent press — do you have any?"

He got up. "Yeah, as a matter of fact. Thanks." He went into his room to get it.

"Would you do my laundry, too?" Buddy asked. "If I asked you nicely?"

"If you *paid* me nicely, sure," Jamie said.

"How about a dollar a load?"

She nodded. "That'll get you the *rinse cycle*."

"No spin?" he asked.

She shook her head. "No spin. No dry. No fold."

"Maybe I'll do it myself," he said.

She nodded. "Good call."

Charles came out with a small armload of shirts and a pair of jeans, handing all of it to her. "Thanks — I owe you one."

She grinned. "Okay."

Buddy flipped through the chapter he was supposed to be reading in his textbook. "You know something, Charles? The legislative process is *dull*."

"No," Charles said. "*Differential equations are dull*."

"Have you decided to take it Pass/Fail?"

Charles nodded.

"Think you'll pass?"

"I'd *better*," Charles said, flipping to the next page in his paper.

Mr. Powell came through on his way to the kitchen, nodding briefly at them, both boys nodding back.

"He doesn't like me much," Buddy said.

"No, he's just into being gruff." Charles put an accent over the first "e" in "détente." "Especially with guys our age."

"Who ate all the cake?" Mr. Powell bellowed from the kitchen.

"You think he's going to come out here and click ball bearings together?" Buddy asked.

Charles laughed. "He's only yelling because you're here. If you weren't, he'd just go find Adam and accuse him of it."

Mr. Powell came out to the living room. "Lembeck! Did you eat that cake?"

"No, Captain Queeg," Buddy said solemnly. "I didn't."

Mr. Powell tried to look stern, but cracked a smile. "I *see*," he said, and went back into the kitchen.

"You *did* eat most of it," Charles said.

Buddy lifted his hands in pretended innocence. "Hey, you ate your share, too. Besides, we left some."

"Oh, yeah," Charles said. "Lots."

Adam came out of the den. "Is it nine yet, Charles?"

Charles looked at his watch. "Ten of."

Adam sighed, sitting down on the couch. "I wish he'd call early."

"Well, I think it must be pretty hard to get a call through from there," Charles said. "So, he *has* to plan it in advance."

"Yeah." Adam sighed again. "I guess." He watched Charles read the last two pages of his paper and Buddy flip pages in his book. "Are you guys getting a lot done?"

"Always," Buddy said. "A night doesn't pass that Charles and I don't get three — four! — hours of studying in."

Charles lifted an eyebrow at him. "Make that three or four *minutes*."

"Hey, just because you're a slacker . . ." Buddy said. He clapped a hand on Adam's shoulder. "Remember, son. Work hard, play hard, sleep well at night."

"You forgot 'eat from the four basic food

groups,' " Charles said, and Adam laughed.

Sarah came in from the den, too, glanced at the phone, then sat down on the couch next to Adam.

"Have you guys ever heard the expression "A watched pot never boils'?" Charles asked.

They both nodded.

"Do you maybe want to quiz me for a minute?" Sarah asked.

Charles put his paper down. "Okay." He closed his eyes, trying to remember a few lines. " 'Thou still unravish'd bride of quietness, Thou foster-child of silence and slow time.' "

"Um — Keats," Sarah said.

"Oh, very good," Charles said. "Thought I'd get you with that."

"Can you quiz me, too?" Adam asked.

"Okay." Charles thought again. "Whose record for saves did Dave Righetti break?"

"Quisenberry," Adam said without hesitating. "He had forty-five."

Buddy just stared at them. "Is this what you guys *do* all the time?"

Charles shrugged. "Now and again."

"Why don't you just spring for a game of Trivial Pursuit?"

"Too predictable," Charles said, trying to think of another poem. If it wouldn't defeat the purpose of the whole thing, he would write them down and make life a little easier. "Oh, I've got one. 'Between the dark and the daylight, When the night is beginning to lower, Comes a pause in the day's occupations, That is known as the Children's Hour.' "

Sarah grinned. "Henry Wadsworth Longfellow."

"Oh, you're too smart for me." He turned to Adam. "What pitcher had the nickname, The Big Train?"

"Walter Johnson," Adam said. "Because he threw so hard."

"Okay." He turned to Sarah. "Now, for a special bonus, who wrote a *play* called *The Children's Hour*?"

"Um —" Sarah frowned, stumped. "Um —"

"Lillian Hellman," Buddy said unexpectedly.

They all turned to look at him.

"Sorry," he said. "Got carried away."

"No, no, that's good," Charles said, and looked at Adam. "Who hit the home run that *tied* the sixth game of the seventy-five World Series?"

"Oh." Adam blinked. "Well — Carlton Fisk's homer *won* it."

Charles nodded. "But who *tied* it?"

Adam shook his head. "I don't know."

"Can I answer?" Buddy asked.

Charles laughed. "Sure."

"Bernie Carbo, right?"

Charles nodded. "Looks like we have a winner, kids."

"Hunh." Buddy looked pleased with himself. "What do I get?"

"Our heartfelt congratulations," Charles said.

"That's *it*?"

"Sorry," Charles said.

The phone rang, and Sarah and Adam both sat up straighter.

"Sarah? Adam? Jamie?" Mrs. Powell called down the stairs. "Your father's on the phone!"

They both jumped up, and Jamie came hurrying out of the kitchen, Mr. Powell right behind her, all of them trooping upstairs.

"I *really* don't get a prize?" Buddy said.

Charles laughed. "Sorry."

"I *should* get a prize." Buddy looked toward the kitchen. "Think they have any cookies in there?"

"Yeah." Charles grinned, standing up. "Let's go."

Chapter 12

The next night, Mr. Powell had his regular poker game and Mrs. Powell went out with friends from work, so Charles took the kids out for pizza at Sid's.

"Be cool," Jamie said to her brother and sister as they sat down. "There are *college* people here."

"We're always cool," Sarah said, fixing her hair ribbon.

"We *invented* cool," Adam said, and blew a very large bubble with his gum, popping it with a loud, attention-attracting snap.

"Okay, okay," Charles said, sensing potential trouble here. "Let's not bicker. We're here to have a lovely time, right?"

"*Lovely*," Adam said, and snickered.

Jamie stood up, having apparently decided to rise above all of this. "Can I go see what's on the jukebox, Charles?"

He gave her three quarters. "Just don't play the Beach Boys. Sid *hates* the Beach Boys."

"I *hate* the Beach Boys," Sid said, suddenly at their table with his order pad. "Hey, Charles. Nice to see you hanging out with these respectable types."

"Sarah, Adam, and Jamie," Charles said, pointing to each in turn. "This is Sid, guys."

Sarah and Adam's hellos were shy; Jamie's as sophisticated as she could manage. She paused before going over to the jukebox.

"Do you hate Duran Duran?" she asked.

"Well." Sid's sigh was extra deep. " 'Wild Boys' would be all right, I guess."

"What about a-ha?" she asked.

He shook his head. "I don't think so."

Charles laughed. "What a tyrant."

"Absolute power corrupts absolutely." Sid took a pen from behind his ear. "What can I get for all of you?"

"Anything you guys want," Jamie said and went over to the jukebox.

"She's on a *very* strict diet," Adam explained to Sid.

Sid laughed. "Well, I'll tell you this much. I got some Vidalia onions, so my special today's those with the *finest* red and green peppers, the odd chunk of pineapple, and the *best* fresh sausage."

Charles pretended to look confused. "Wh-what's odd about the pineapple?"

"He's being *poetic*," Sarah said.

"*Told* you she was classy, Charles," Sid said. "And if you ask me nicely, I just might slice up an artichoke heart or two."

Adam made a face. "Sounds kind of weird."

"Taste it, friend," Sid said. "You won't be making a mistake."

Charles nodded. "Okay, we'll go for one of those —"

Sid interrupted him. "Don't forget the asking me nicely part."

Charles grinned. "Sid, old buddy, old pal, will you please, out of the kindness of your heart, and the artistry of your soul, make us one Special pizza, and one with pepperoni?"

Sid took a step backward. "*Plain* pepperoni?"

Charles looked at Adam, who nodded gratefully. "I think so, yeah."

"Well," Sid wrote it down, "since you asked me nicely." He looked up. "Anything to slake your thirst?"

"Could I have orange, please?" Sarah asked.

"Me, too," Adam said.

"I'll have a Coke and" — Charles indicated Jamie — "she'll have *anything* with Nutrasweet."

Sid nodded, writing it down. He started for the kitchen, but paused as he saw Jamie returning to the table. "So. What do I have to look forward to?"

"Springsteen?" she said tentatively.

He nodded. "Always happy to have Bruce in here. What else?"

" 'Wild Boys,' 'When Doves Cry,' and 'Love for Sale.' "

"Thank you for the Talking Heads," he said, very solemn.

"Um, you're welcome," she said, sitting down.

"Back before you know it," he said, and went to the kitchen.

"Glory Days" started playing and they could hear Sid's shouted, "All right!" from the kitchen.

"Do you and Buddy come here a lot?" Adam asked, looking around.

Charles nodded. "Mostly always."

"Do you bring girls here?" Jamie asked.

Charles nodded again. "Generally."

"You should have *seen* the girls I met," Sarah said. "What was the name of the one with you, Charles? Buffy?"

"Patti," he said. "And they were very nice girls."

Sarah giggled.

Jamie leaned forward, obviously about ready to giggle herself. "So, wait. What were they like?"

"You know how Mom takes one look at you sometimes and says you can't leave the house?" Sarah asked.

Jamie nodded.

"*That's* what they looked like," Sarah said.

"*I* think we should change the subject," Charles said.

"What did we order, anyway?" Jamie asked.

"Thank you," Charles said. "Pepperoni and Sid's Special."

"With *artichokes*," Adam said.

Jamie shuddered. "Gross."

"Don't let Sid hear you say that," Charles said. "Besides, it tastes better than you'd think."

"What's a Vidalia onion, anyway?" Sarah asked.

Charles shrugged. "Extra special kind, I guess."

"What?" Adam let his mouth fall open. "There's things you don't know?"

"Afraid so," Charles said.

"Like," Adam's voice was extra casual, "the year Ted Williams had his best batting average?"

The *year*? "He hit .406," Charles said.

Adam smiled. "When?"

"Uh — " He had no idea, except that it would have been the 1940s or 1950s — "Nineteen forty-six?"

"Nineteen forty-one," Adam said, only slightly smug.

"Hunh." Charles moved his jaw. "Been waiting all day to ask me that?"

Adam nodded, grinning.

"Hunh," Charles said.

Sid came out with their sodas and then, the pizzas, depositing them on the table with a flourish, along with a stack of plates and napkins.

"It looks really good," Sarah said, reaching for a piece of Sid's Special.

"Classy kid," Sid said to Charles. "Very classy kid. Wait a minute," he said, lifting the pepperoni pizza out of the way as Jamie and Adam reached for it. "You at least have to *try* the other one."

Jamie hesitated, but took a piece of the Special. She tasted it cautiously, then with more enthusiasm. "That *is* good."

Sid looked pleased. "You may play a-ha."

"What about Tears for Fears?" she asked.

"Don't push your luck." He folded his arms, waiting for Charles and Adam to try it, too.

"Not bad," Adam said, after tasting Sarah's.

"La pièce de résistance," Charles said.

Sid grinned and gave Jamie a quarter. "Tears for Fears," he said. "On the house."

At their next psychology class, Charles and Buddy were on their best behavior, not even sitting together. Dr. Feinberg noticed this, and her only comment was, "Divide and conquer, boys?" The rest of the class found this quite amusing.

After class, Buddy came over, grabbing Charles's arm. "Come on."

Charles pulled back, suspicious. "Where?"

"Just come with me." Buddy dragged him down to where their professor was putting her books and papers into her briefcase to leave.

"Buddy," Charles tried to pull away, "I really don't — "

"*Trust* me," Buddy said.

"That's probably what *Custer* said."

Charles was going to escape, but Dr. Feinberg had already seen them.

"Yes?" she asked pleasantly.

As Charles considered his options — run away as fast as his legs could carry him, fall into a dead faint and wait for the Emergency Rescue Squad, transfer to another college — Buddy, with a big smile, reached inside his knapsack, taking out a very shiny apple.

"A gift," he said.

The side of their professor's mouth twitched slightly. "How thoughtful," she said.

"It's a Cortland," he said. "Particularly delicious."

"Well, thank you." She put it in her brief-case.

Hoping that that was it, Charles turned to go.

"*Not* so fast," Buddy said, both Charles and Dr. Feinberg stopping in midmovement. He reached into his knapsack, taking out three apples. He handed them to her with a bigger smile. "For a pie."

She laughed and Charles groaned, covering his eyes with his hand.

"Buddy, could we *please* leave now?" he asked.

Buddy beamed. "Certainly."

"Excuse us," Charles said to their professor. "He was raised by jackals."

Dr. Feinberg just laughed.

When they were out in the hall, Charles stopped.

"Are you *completely* crazy, Buddy?" he asked.

"No, she likes us now," Buddy said. "I could tell."

"For a pie, Buddy? A *pie*?"

"Trust me." Buddy opened the outside door. "One day you'll thank me for that."

Charles shook his head, following him. "One day I'll break your neck."

"Oh, hey," Buddy said, unfazed. "Feel like playing some hoop after my one o'clock?"

"Sure," Charles said, then smiled his best evil smile. "Bring a neck brace."

"You know what I think?" Buddy said, dribbling toward the basket as they played one-on-one later that afternoon.

Charles stayed with him, forcing him to reverse and dribble back toward the foul line. "Since when do you think?"

Buddy feinted left, saw that Charles hadn't gone for it, and kept dribbling. "Are you still mad about the apples?"

"*Yes.*"

Buddy dribbled up to the top of the key, keeping his body between Charles and the ball. "*I* still think it was a smart move."

"You ever going to shoot?" Charles asked.

"I'm thinking, okay?"

"No pressure," Charles said, and slapped at the ball, almost knocking it free. As Buddy kept dribbling, he lost patience and went for the ball again, Buddy easily driving past him for a lay-up.

"Sucker," Buddy said, catching the ball as it came through the basket, and bringing it out past the foul line. "Anyway — " He stopped dribbling and took a long shot, the ball bouncing off the rim, Charles retrieving it.

"Anyway?" Charles said, dribbling out to the foul line.

"Oh, right." Buddy moved in to guard him. "I was thinking that we don't meet enough girls."

"I don't know." Charles faked right and went left, driving for the basket. He made the shot and took the ball back out. "Seems like we have a lot of lunch companions."

"Yeah, but — I don't know." Buddy shook his head. "I'm kind of worried about Sophomore Slump."

"Well, what about those girls?" Charles indicated the door with his eyes.

"Where?" Buddy turned and Charles dribbled in for a lay-up. "Hey!" Buddy turned back. "That's not fair!"

Charles caught the ball. "You know what my coach would say?"

"Keep your head in the game," Buddy said, sighing.

Charles grinned. "We must have had the same coach."

"Anyway," Buddy guarded him, "I just think we should like, make an effort."

"Funny," Charles faked right again, but it didn't work this time, "I never thought that *particular* thing was a problem."

"I don't know." Buddy knocked the ball away, but Charles was able to get it back. "I guess what I really mean is instead of going out with like, as many girls as we can, we should maybe try to meet a couple we really like."

Charles stopped dribbling. "You're not getting *sensitive*, are you?"

"No!" Buddy said. "I just — forget it, I was just thinking."

"What's the deal? You have someone in mind?"

"I don't know," Buddy said. "I mean, there's this girl in my Marine Biology class — but, I don't know — she's probably too smart. I mean — you think I should give it a shot? Like talk to her, maybe?"

Charles laughed. "Sounds pretty intense." He started to dribble again, remembering just too late that that would be a double-dribble.

"Thank you," Buddy said, taking the ball from him.

Charles switched positions with him. "Don't mention it."

Buddy drove in hard, then stopped, trying a fade-away jump shot. The shot missed, and they scuffled for the rebound, Buddy coming up with it and dribbling back out past the foul line again.

"You think I'm out to lunch with this get-to-know-girls-better routine?" he asked.

"I think you're just *generally* out to

lunch," Charles said, and shook his head. *"Pie."*

Buddy laughed and dribbled toward the net, trying a hook shot that went right past the blackboard and out-of-bounds.

"Thank you," Charles said, bringing the ball back.

Buddy grinned wryly. "Don't mention it."

Chapter 13

Upon further reflection, Charles decided that Buddy was right: They were in sort of a dry spell. Or, at any rate, a rut. They *did* need more women in their lives. "Women" being the operative word, as opposed to "girls." Although, in his opinion, there should be a word between the two words, like "guys" was the stage between "boys" and "men." "Gals" just didn't work somehow.

Asking someone more serious out was probably a valid idea, too. He had spent most of freshman year going out with a girl who was both bright *and* beautiful, and since they'd broken up, he had been going out with — well, less challenging girls. Not necessarily conversationalists. Heidi and Patti being excellent examples of that.

But it *was* time to ask out someone more well-rounded. Someone who wasn't much for giggling, someone — someone like Rachel in his foreign policy class. He'd never said more than hello to her because — he wasn't sure why now that he thought of it. Because she wasn't overtly his type? Quiet, neat, long dark hair. Not going out of her way to participate in class, but not afraid to be intelligent when she did. Very thoughtful, very self-contained. Actually, he probably hadn't talked to her much because all of that was pretty intimidating.

Today, though, today he would make an effort. There weren't any assigned seats or anything, so he'd just get there a little early and sit near the part of the room where she usually sat. Then, he'd think of a couple of intelligent things to say — both to her, and in class. Or — maybe Sarah's poetry would come in handy. He could sing of brooks; of blossoms, birds, and bowers — maybe not. Maybe he should just talk about *Nightline* or something.

He got to the classroom ten minutes early, heading right for the desk where she usually — except that she was already there, at a desk near the back, bent over a book. They were the only two in the room, and he stopped in confusion, not sure if he should veer over the other way, or stick to his guns, or —

"Guess we're both here pretty early," she said, closing her book, using her finger as a bookmark.

"Uh — yeah," he said, still standing in the middle of the room. Decision. Make a decision. It was too obvious to sit right next to her, so he chose a seat diagonally across from her. Intelligent. Think of something intelligent to say. He opened his knapsack to get his notebook, still thinking. "Uh, this is a pretty good class."

She nodded.

What a stupid thing to say. Maybe she *hated* the class. Now she would think he was a jerk. "I mean," he coughed, "you know, so far." Leaving the possibility that the class could get *lousy* any minute now.

"Yeah," she said.

Terrific. She thought he was a total idiot — he could tell. Instead of intelligent remarks, the best he had come up with was insipid. Embarrassed, he opened *The New York Times* he had intentionally brought with him. He *did* read it sometimes, but not as regularly as carrying it around made it look.

She cleared her throat slightly. "Did you see that half the Jets' offensive line is on injured reserve?" she asked, indicating the newspaper.

He was in love. "Well, I'm a Steelers' man," he said.

"Because you wanted to be Bradshaw or because you're from Pennsylvania?"

"I'm from Pennsylvania," he said.

She nodded. "I'm from New York."

"The city?"

She nodded.

Instead of finding that intimidating, he decided to ask another question. "You're not a *Yankees*' fan, are you?"

She laughed. "No, my parents are from

New England, so we're Red Sox people."

Like still being a Brooklyn Dodgers' fan, being a Red Sox fan was *always* acceptable. One of life's little constants. "I guess you hate the Mets now, too?" he guessed.

"I *always* hated the Mets," she said.

"They were pretty swell in nineteen sixty-nine," he said.

She shook her head. "If we rooted for anyone else, it would be the Dodgers, and not since they left New York."

Would this girl *marry* him maybe? "Hunh," he said, and grinned. Buddy was a genius. Except he had to think of something to say, before she lost interest. "Um, what are you reading?" he asked.

Surprisingly, she blushed. "Oh, I — nothing, really, I — "

What *was* she reading? Intrigued now, he inclined his head just enough to try and see the cover.

"See, I figure if I don't read fun stuff sometimes, I'll end up not — " She sighed, and turned the front of the book so he could see it.

He laughed. Rona Jaffe. "I thought it was going to be Sidney Sheldon or something."

She also smiled. "I just want a *little* escapism, nothing *that* major."

He nodded. "Beach books."

"Yeah."

More people were coming in now, and as the noise level made it harder to hold a conversation, Charles began to feel shy again.

"Oh, I'm Rachel," she said.

"I'm Charles," he said.

Their professor had come in now, and was getting ready to start his lecture, so they just exchanged smiles, Charles feeling about as shy as he could ever remember. Although he usually enjoyed the class, he was too distracted to pay much attention, glancing diagonally ahead whenever he thought he wouldn't get caught.

He liked the way she dressed, he decided. Nothing particularly trendy about it, but she wasn't trying to impress anyone, either. That took maturity, he decided. And just having her hair all nice and smooth like that, instead of fooling around with mousse or whatever. And just *one* earring in each ear, simple ones at that. And — everyone was getting up, and he realized that class was over. He had to think of something to say, something — something memorable, something —

"See you around," Rachel said, passing him on her way out.

"Uh, right," he said, unprepared. He was going to go after her, but that would be too obvious, so he stayed in his seat, pretending to be finishing up some notes. Not that the ones he had taken made much sense.

Noticing that almost everyone had left the room, he gathered his notebook and books together, putting them into his knapsack and swinging it onto his shoulder. Not a bad start. His performance had been a little ragged around the edges, but — on the whole — not a bad start. Not bad at all.

"So, you went for it, hunh?" Buddy said, as they moved through the cafeteria line at lunch.

"Yeah." Charles took a cheeseburger. "She's really nice."

Buddy took *two* cheeseburgers. "You going to ask her out?"

Charles looked at Buddy's tray, then took another cheeseburger. "Well, not *today*."

Buddy took a third cheeseburger. "You mean, you're afraid she might say no."

"I didn't say that."

Buddy grinned at him.

"Okay," Charles admitted. "I'm afraid she would say no." He started to reach for another cheeseburger, then stopped. "Are you *really* going to eat three?"

"Probably not," Buddy said. "Want to split the extra one?"

Charles nodded, taking some french fries.

Buddy took some onion rings. "I guess I'll give it a try, too."

"The girl in Marine Biology?"

Buddy nodded. "I don't have it until tomorrow, so I can figure out good stuff to say."

"Is she smart?" Charles selected both cake and pudding.

Buddy just took cake. Three pieces. "I think so, yeah."

"She probably thinks you are, too."

"Maybe," Buddy said, and laughed. "I guess the reality'll be kind of upsetting."

Charles laughed, too. "Break it to her gently."

"I will, son," Buddy said. "I will."

When Charles got home to the Powells' house that afternoon, he found a pair of legs under the sink. Attached to someone, he hoped.

He put his knapsack on the kitchen table. "Hello?"

The legs moved and there was a dull thud. "Ow," Mr. Powell said.

"Is there something wrong with the sink?"

Mr. Powell brought his head out to look at him. "No, I just find it peaceful under here."

"Well," Charles grinned, "I've always been pretty fond of cupboards, too. I mean, nothing beats a *laundry hamper*, but —"

Mr. Powell did not appear to be amused. "Could I give you a hand, sir?"

Mr. Powell disappeared back underneath the sink. "No, no, I think I've got it."

There was more banging and clinking, then he came up.

"*There*," he said with some satisfaction. He turned on the faucet, water spurting out in all directions. Quickly, he turned it off, but not before getting drenched.

Charles tried not to grin, but didn't have much success. "Maybe it just needs a new washer, sir."

Mr. Powell did not look amused.

"Um, what was *wrong* with it, sir?"

"I don't know — water pressure." Mr. Powell sighed. "Maybe it *was* the washer." He bent down to look at the pipes, then straightened up, shaking his head. "Know anything about plumbing, sailor?"

"Sorry," Charles said. "I was only being polite when I offered."

Mr. Powell nodded, staring at the sink with his hands on his hips.

"Um, the Pembrokes had a pretty good plumber, sir. If you wanted, I could — ?"

Mr. Powell sighed again. "What's his number?"

After looking up the number, Charles handed it to him, then escaped into the living room. All three Powell kids were sitting on the couch.

"Did he fix it yet?" Sarah asked.

"No," Charles said, "but that doesn't mean — "

"He *hates* it when he can't fix things," Jamie said.

Sarah nodded. "Remember the time with the blender?"

That sounded like a potentially ugly story, and Charles decided not to pursue it.

"What about the Etch-a-Sketch," Adam said.

He *really* wasn't going to pursue that one.

There was some very loud banging in the kitchen, followed by a crash, and they all flinched.

"Do you think he's all right?" Charles asked.

Sarah nodded. "I just think we should maybe get out of here."

"Maybe we should get out of *town*," Jamie said.

There were several noisy clangs and some muffled mumbling.

Charles opened the front door. "How about a little hike around the block?"

"Sounds great," Jamie said, following him.

Sarah jumped up. "I'm coming, too."

"Wait for me!" Adam said.

Chapter 14

The plumber fixed the sink.

On Wednesday, Charles seriously considered skipping his Abnormal Psychology class, but Buddy talked him out of it.

"She likes us now," he said. "I swear."

"How do *you* know?" Charles asked.

"I could tell. Honest."

"Unh-hunh," Charles said, but went to the class.

They sat together in their usual seats, and Dr. Feinberg neither smiled nor frowned at them, simply giving her lecture.

"See?" Buddy whispered. "I *told* you."

"We got off lucky," Charles said.

Buddy grinned. "Well, it's not like we have *grades* yet."

Charles scowled at him. But, when class was over and nothing had happened, he decided that the whole thing really *had* blown over, and — Buddy elbowed him, hard.

Charles elbowed him back. "What?"

Buddy indicated the front of the auditorium. "I think she wants us."

"What?" Charles looked, and saw that Dr. Feinberg was motioning for them to come down there. "Oh, great."

"It might not be anything bad."

"That's what *you* — "

"Boys?" Dr. Feinberg said.

They walked down to the front, both scuffing their feet a little.

"Ah." She opened her briefcase, taking out two small, plastic-wrapped paper plates. "Here you go."

Charles stared. *"Pie?"*

"Is that *the* pie, ma'am?" Buddy asked, grinning.

She didn't answer, taking out two plastic forks, then closing the briefcase and putting on her raincoat. "Enjoy," she said, and left.

"I believe she won that round," Buddy said thoughtfully.

"She won the whole *fight*, Buddy."

Buddy nodded, pulling a chair up to the front table and unwrapping his plate.

"You're going to eat it?" Charles said.

"Well, yeah." Buddy picked up his fork. "It looks good."

It *did* look good. Charles pulled a chair up, too.

"Maybe we should bring her some chocolate chips and sugar and stuff," Buddy said.

Charles had to laugh. "Shut up and eat your pie, Buddy."

"It's good," Buddy said, his mouth full.

It was *very* good.

In the excitement of the pie and all, Charles was almost late to his foreign policy class. He made it just in time, but the only empty seats were up in the front. He smiled hello at Rachel as he made his way up to the front, and she smiled back. Which was encouraging.

This time, when class was over, he jumped right up, timing it so that they would be going through the door at the same time.

"Hi," he said.

"Hi," she said. "How are you?"

He liked her sweater. It was a very nice sweater. Fair Isle, he thought they were called. "Um, how are you?" he asked.

"Fine, thanks," she said.

"That's a very nice sweater."

She laughed. "Thank you."

He nodded. Think of something more interesting. "Are you — going to class now?"

She nodded. "European Novel."

"Is that in Downing?" Which was the name of the English building.

"Yeah," she said.

"May I — walk you there?"

She grinned. "Okay."

They walked outside, Charles's mind a complete blank as far as conversation topics were concerned.

"When do you think we'll get our papers back?" she asked.

"Foreign policy?" Charles asked, then wanted to slap himself. What *other* papers would she mean? They only had one class together. "I don't know. Pretty soon, I hope." This conversation was going from dull to duller. "Do you like your English class?" Oh, yeah, great improvement.

She shrugged. "It's okay. I could do without Thomas Mann."

"I'm in Shakespeare this semester."

"Do you like it?"

He grinned, and they kept walking.

"Is it just me," he asked, "or were we having a slightly more glib conversation the other day?"

"I think we were," she said.

He nodded, but then promptly heard himself asking, "What are you majoring in?"

"I don't know yet," she said. "Probably English. You?"

"I don't know yet," he said. "Definitely *not* economics."

She nodded. "I know what you mean — they're pretty hard-core down there."

"I think they're even worse than premed."

"Computer people," she said. "Computer people are getting *really* cutthroat."

"That's true." He looked up ahead — he could see Downing Hall now, but they still had a little time left. If he could think of anything to say. "So, uh, how *do* you think the Jets look this year?"

"Well," she shook her head, "I'd take O'Brien over just about anyone, but I don't think they have the depth." She grinned. "What about the Steelers?"

"It's a building year," he said, and she laughed. "Did you, um, play on teams in high school?"

"The *chess* team," she said.

"Were you good?"

She shrugged. "I had a pretty good Queen's Gambit."

That struck him funny, and he laughed.

"I did," she said.

"I'm sure you did," he said, still laughing. "It just sounds like — I don't know — you had 'good hands' or something."

She laughed, too. "Did you play a lot of sports in high school?"

He nodded.

"Good hands?" she asked.

"Good *wheels*."

She laughed. "Jock-talk kills me."

They were in front of Downing Hall now.

He looked at his watch. "I'm sorry, I hope you're not late."

She looked at her watch, too. "I think I'll just make it." She started up the steps. "Thank you for walking me."

"Um, Rachel?"

She paused.

"I was wondering — that is — I mean, I — " spit it out, Charles — "well, I thought — are you busy Friday night?"

"I don't think so," she said, and grinned. "Why?"

"Oh, no reason," he said.

She continued up the steps.

She was putting him on, right? Or maybe — "Would you like to go out to dinner? And a movie?"

She stopped, and he could tell from her grin that she *had* been putting him on. "Yes, I would," she said.

"Where do you live?"

"Cavanaugh. Room two-oh-eight."

"Say — six-thirty?" he said.

She smiled. "Sounds great."

"Well, then — then, I'll see you then," he said.

"You're not coming to class on Friday?"

Right. "I'll see you then, too," he said.

The campus chapel bell began to ring, and they both looked at their watches.

"See you Friday," she said.

"Great," he said, and stood there, grinning foolishly, until she was gone.

"She *did*?" Buddy said at lunch. "Way to go!"

Charles shrugged an "it was nothing" shrug.

"You fall all over your words asking her?"

Yes. "No," Charles said.

"I *know* you're lying," Buddy said, picking up his Sloppy Joe.

"Yeah."

"I *knew* it." Buddy took a bite, half of the filling falling out onto his plate.

"So, do you really like her?" Buddy asked.

Charles nodded. "I think so, yeah." Who was he kidding? "I mean, yeah, I do."

Buddy gave up on trying to eat the Sloppy

Joe as a sandwich and picked up a fork. "What's she like?"

"Well . . . kind of preppy, I guess. Smart. She likes sports, too."

"You mean, she's a jock?"

"I don't think so," Charles said, still not sure. "She just seems to like sports, not actually *play* them."

"Is she pretty?"

Charles nodded. "Yeah. Very — smooth-looking."

"You glad you asked her?"

"Yeah," Charles said. "Totally."

Buddy lowered his fork, obviously not enjoying his sandwich. "I have Marine Biology next — think I should go for it, too?"

"Absolutely," Charles said, all confidence now that he had already gotten the hard part over with.

"You want to double?"

Did he? No, not on a first date. "No," Charles said. "Let's see how it works out first."

Buddy opened the second of his three milks. "You're probably right. She might not say yes to me, anyway."

"Sure she will," Charles said.

"Well, I *hope* so." Buddy looked at his barely touched Sloppy Joe, then at Charles's grinder with one bite taken out of it. "I don't know about you, but I *hate* my lunch."

"Me, too," Charles said.

"Feel like switching?"

Charles was already exchanging plates. "Love to," he said.

Although he had promised Mrs. Powell that he would do the grocery shopping for her that afternoon, Charles had *also* promised Buddy that he would wait for him in the student union to find out if he'd had the guts to ask for the date or not.

He sat on the floor by the student activities bulletin board, and was just starting to get impatient when Buddy came swaggering over.

"Turned you down, hunh?" he said.

Buddy swaggered around some more. "She said she'd *love* to."

"All *right*," Charles said. Two for two. Not a bad day. "Where you going to go?"

"The movies, on Saturday."

"Oh," Charles said, and grinned. "We're going to dinner, *and* the movies."

Buddy ignored the implication. "Which movie you going to — we can run into you."

Charles shook his head. "We're going Friday."

"Good," Buddy said. "If whatever you see's really bad, or really good, you can tell me."

"Do my best," Charles said, getting up.

"You have time to play some hoop?" Buddy did a jump-shot toward the wall.

"I can't — I told Mrs. Powell I'd do some stuff for her."

Buddy shrugged. "I'll walk as far as the gym with you."

Charles nodded, lifting his knapsack onto his shoulder. On their way out, he paused by the water fountain to get a drink. "So." He straightened up. "What's *your* date like?"

"*Really* cool," Buddy said. "I mean, you know me, I'm pretty cool, but this girl — I can maybe *learn* from this girl."

"Does she think you're a brain?"

"Well — " Buddy's expression was doubtful. "I think she thinks I'm fun."

"Is *she* smart?"

Buddy nodded. "Oh, yeah. She got an A on the research thing, too."

"Match made in heaven," Charles said, amused. "You two can open your bait shop *together*."

"*You* two can coach together," Buddy said.

"Yeah, *right*," Charles said. Although. . . .

They were at the gym now, and Buddy stopped.

"Well, catch you later, cowboy." Buddy reached out to shake Charles's hand. "Good work today."

Charles grinned. "You, too."

"Sophomore Slump is a thing of our past."

"*Distant* past," Charles said.

Chapter 15

Charles had been in a pretty good mood to begin with, and by the time he got to the Powells' house — after kicking a few rocks, and even running a stick along part of a fence — he was in a great mood.

He went in through the back door, letting it slam shut behind him. Sarah and Jamie were at the table, reading the latest letter from their father.

"Hi, guys!" he said. "How's tricks?"

"You're in a pretty good mood," Jamie said.

"I'm in a *great* mood." He checked the mail to see if he had gotten anything, and the fact that he hadn't didn't even bother him. "What's your father have to say?"

"That he misses us, mostly," Sarah said.

"He *also* wants to know how you're working out," Jamie said.

"Well, tell him the sad truth: I can take it." He leaned into the living room. "Hey, Adam! You —" He saw that Adam was right there, tying his shoes, and that he needn't bellow. "Adam," he said, in a calmer voice. "Feel like coming shopping with us?"

Jamie perked up. "Shopping where?"

"*Grocery* shopping," Charles said. "*Then,* we're going to cook the bestest, swellest — "

Sarah snapped her fingers. "You asked that girl out, right?"

"I certainly did," Charles said.

"And she said, 'Certainly'?" Adam guessed.

"She certainly did." Charles grabbed the car keys, list, and money Mrs. Powell had left on the counter for him. "Everyone ready to go?"

"Do we *have* to?" Jamie asked.

"Yes."

"Even if — " Sarah started.

"Even if," Charles said. "Come on." To his surprise, they all followed him out to the car without arguing.

"I call front!" Sarah said.

"I call it on the way home!" Adam said.

"I call it *both* ways next time," Jamie said.

"Everyone happy now?" Charles asked, and they all nodded. "Good."

Once they were inside the grocery store, Charles leaned on the handle of the shopping cart, studying the list.

"Mom?" Adam yanked on his sweat shirt. "Can we get Twinkies?"

"No, son." He looked at Sarah. "It says 'paper products.' What does that mean?"

She shrugged. "Paper towels, paper plates, paper cups —"

"Got it," he said. "You want to be responsible for that?"

She nodded, heading for that aisle.

"Is this going to be, like, a team effort?" Jamie asked.

"Yup," Charles said. "Go get eggs, milk, and butter."

She frowned. "That lacked a magic word."

"Please," he said.

She sighed an extremely deep sigh. "Very well."

"Should I go get the Pop-Tarts and the Ring Dings, Mom?" Adam asked.

Charles shook his head. "You may get the oatmeal and the Grape-Nuts, son."

"We don't get to get *anything* fun?"

"No."

"What a grinch," Adam said.

Charles nodded. "You know it."

They bought detergent and sponges, waxed paper and trash bags. Fruit and vegetables, hamburger and chicken. Vegetable oil, baking soda, soy sauce. Orange juice, Coke, coffee.

Sarah shook her head, looking at the basket. "Did Mom write down *all* boring stuff?"

Charles nodded, checking over the list to make sure they had everything. "Pretty much."

"Can we get cake?" Adam asked. "We *always* get cake."

They *did* always get cake. "Sure," Charles

said. Why not. Someone took his hand and he glanced over, surprised to see that it was Jamie. "Jamie, what are you — "

"Oh, come on, honey," she said, her voice extra loud. "We *always* get decaffeinated."

He tried to pull his hand free, but she clung to it more tightly. "What is this," he said, "some sort of weird parody?"

"Oh, honey." She laughed. "You say the *cutest* things."

"Hello, Jamie," a woman coming up the aisle said, sounding surprised.

Jamie looked up in even greater surprise. "Oh, hi, Mrs. Corcoran." She leaned against Charles's arm. "This is *Charles*."

Not able to think of any graceful way out of this, Charles smiled weakly. "Hello, ma'am."

"Hello," she said, obviously not approving. "See you tomorrow, Jamie."

As she turned down another aisle, Jamie dropped his hand, laughing.

"*Tell* me that wasn't one of your teachers," Charles said.

Jamie just laughed.

"That was a *really* obnoxious thing to do."

She nodded, laughing.

"I should go after her and tell her the truth."

"Oh, I don't think you should go after her, Charles. She didn't seem to like you much."

Remembering her teacher's expression, Charles had to laugh, too. "I guess you think you're pretty funny."

"Hilarious," she said.

"Obnoxious," he said. "Don't do that again."

"Never ever," she said, and laughed some more.

When they got home and had unpacked the groceries, Charles opened the refrigerator again to try and decide what to have for dinner.

"How about meatloaf?" he suggested.

Adam rolled his eyes. "Yum, yum."

"No, the kind I make is really good." He started taking out ingredients. "And you guys can make a salad, and we'll have some baked potatoes, and — I don't know. Garlic bread?"

They all nodded or shrugged.

It was a team effort, with plenty of mild bickering along the way.

"Eggs in our meatloaf?" Jamie said, watching him make it.

"Always," Charles said, throwing away the two shells. "And oatmeal instead of bread crumbs — makes all the difference."

Adam made a face as he scrubbed the potatoes. "Sounds gross."

Charles dumped a couple of handfuls of chopped onions and some salt and pepper into the mixture. "Well, it isn't. My mother makes it this way."

The oven light went off, indicating that it had heated to 350 degrees, and Charles got a fork, piercing each potato a couple of times.

"When we had a microwave, and Jamie

didn't do that once, they blew up all over the place," Adam said.

Jamie scowled at him. "*That's* a happy memory."

"Wait," Charles said, as Sarah started to put garlic salt on the split and buttered loaf of French bread. "Let's use *real* garlic — makes — "

"All the difference," she guessed.

He looked sheepish. "Something like that."

When Mrs. Powell came in with their grandfather — lots of times, she picked him up on her way home — the four of them were sitting at the kitchen table, cutting carrots, radishes, and cucumbers into various shapes for the salad.

"What's all this?" Mr. Powell asked, taking off his Navy cap.

"We made dinner," Adam said cheerfully.

Mrs. Powell sniffed the air. "Whatever it is smells great."

"We taught Charles how to make meatloaf," Jamie explained. "He's — well, he's not very good at these things."

"Right, honey," Charles said.

Jamie flushed, and changed the subject. "How was work, Mom?"

Mrs. Powell shrugged, taking a pitcher out of the refrigerator and pouring herself some ice tea. "All right, I guess. Want some, Dad?" she asked Mr. Powell, then poured him some as he nodded.

"How was work for *you*?" Sarah asked him.

"Fair to middlin'," he said. "You youngsters learn much in school today?"

"Lots," Adam said.

"*Amazing* amounts," Jamie said.

"*Everything*," Sarah said.

Charles continued making his radish rose until he realized they were all waiting for his response. "Oh. Well — great things. *Many* things."

"Good to hear it, good to hear it," Mr. Powell said. "You all need a hand?"

Charles shook his head. "We're just about set, sir. It'll be ready in about half an hour."

"In *that* case," Mrs. Powell said, "why don't we go take in the news, Dad?"

"Well — " He hesitated. "*M*A*S*H* is on, you know."

"Why don't we go take in M*A*S*H?"

"You guys can go, too," Charles said, as they left. "I mean, I don't mind if you — "

"I'd rather stay and finish up," Sarah said, giving him a big smile.

The other two nodded, and not about to argue, Charles just smiled back.

"Okay," he said. "What kind of dressing do we want to make?"

"No mustard," Adam said.

"Okay." Charles opened the cupboard, taking out things like spices and vegetable oil and vinegar. "We'll just make it up as we go along." He brought a jar over to the table and they all put different things in — garlic, pepper, lemon juice, a little honey, a little soy

sauce, basil, oregano, that sort of thing —
tasting it every so often.

Finally, they were all satisfied, and Charles
closed the jar, giving it one last shake before
putting it in the refrigerator to chill a bit.

"You know," Jamie remarked, "not to get
sentimental or anything, but I'm kind of
glad you live with us, Charles."

"Me, too," Sarah said.

"*Mo* throo," Adam said.

Charles smiled, sitting back down at the
table with them. "I'm kind of glad, too," he
said.

The next day, Buddy's eleven o'clock section meeting was canceled, and Charles didn't
have a class until one, so they decided to
meet in the game room of the student union
to shoot a little pool.

"How about a little wager?" Buddy suggested, chalking the tip of his stick.

"You've got a date on Saturday," Charles
pointed out. "Don't you want to save your
money?"

"*You're* the one who should be worried,"
Buddy said, then frowned. "You want to
maybe just bet lunch?"

Charles shrugged. "Sounds fair."

"Good." Buddy put the chalk down. "*Rack*
'em."

"How many times did you see *The Color
of Money*?"

"I did the *stunt* work on that, sucker."

"Unh-hunh," Charles said, and set up the balls.

Buddy placed the cue ball on the table, bending to do the break. "You know what's bugging me?"

Charles leaned on the stick he had selected. "Your continuing losing streak to me in all sports?"

Buddy shook his head. "This stupid song I can't get out of my head."

"What song?"

"I don't even know what it's called." Buddy made the break, without much success. So little success, in fact, that it was Charles's turn. "Some girl was humming it in line at breakfast and now I can't get it out of my head."

Charles moved around the table, looking for the best shot. "Do you know the *words* to it?"

"Yeah. Something about mares eating oats, and little lambs having some ivy and all."

Charles winced, instantly knowing the song he meant. "I *hate* that song."

"Yeah, well, imagine having it go through your head all day."

"Now that it *is*, yeah." Charles sighted along his stick. "Side pocket," he said, and made the shot.

Buddy sniffed. "Beginner's luck."

"You want to raise the bet?"

"No."

"Didn't *think* so." Charles moved to find

his next shot, then bent down. "Corner pocket," he said, and made it.

"Do you get *tired* of being good at things all the time?" Buddy asked.

"No," Charles said, finding his next shot. "Corner pocket," he said, and knocked the ball in. Now, though, he didn't have much of a shot *anywhere*, so he gave the cue ball a little tap to give Buddy an even worse angle.

"You're supposed to be my friend," Buddy said. "Not be mean to me."

Charles shrugged. "Just close your eyes — maybe you'll get lucky."

Buddy did — and he didn't. "What movie are you going to tomorrow?"

Charles found a great shot and took advantage of it. "Side pocket," he said, then moved to find the next one. "Probably that new Rob Reiner thing."

"I loved *Spinal Tap*," Buddy said.

"I've liked all his stuff." Charles rubbed some chalk on his stick and bent over the table. "Corner pocket."

"You'll let me know if it's any good, right?" Buddy asked, after he made it. "Or if there's anything *too* embarrassing, or — well, too *anything*?"

Charles nodded. "Sure. Side pocket."

After Charles won the game easily, Buddy sighed.

"Two out of three?" he suggested.

"Sure," Charles said.

After Charles won the next one, Buddy sighed again.

"Three out of five?" he asked.

Charles shrugged. "*Rack* 'em, Surfer-Boy."

After Charles won *that* game, Buddy gave the table a little kick.

"You want to go for four out of seven?" Charles asked.

Buddy shook his head. "I want to go for *lunch*."

"Okay." Charles put his stick away, hung up the rack, dropped the cue ball into a side pocket. "You want to go to the dining hall?"

Buddy thought about that. "No, I'm kind of sick of it. Let's go somewhere else."

"Okay." Charles shrugged again. "Seeing as it's on you."

"How did I *know* you were going to say that?"

"I don't know," Charles said, and grinned. "Psychic, I guess."

Chapter 16

They ended up, big surprise, at Sid's, sitting in their usual booth along the wall.

"Tell you what" — Buddy checked his pockets for quarters — "I'll go put on some tunes."

"Sid'll throw us out of here if you put on the Beach Boys again," Charles said, popping open his Coke.

"It's a ritual, Charles. I *need* rituals in my life."

Charles grinned. "Maybe you should consider divinity school."

"Maybe I'll just stick to knocking on wood." Buddy snapped his fingers. "Which is a great song. I'll put that on, too." He went over to the jukebox, studying the song list as if he hadn't seen it many times before.

Sid brought their pizza over, a large pepperoni with onions. "If he puts on the Beach Boys, Charles. . . ."

"You know he's going to," Charles said.

Sid nodded. "I guess it's good to have things to count on."

"The pizza looks great," Charles said. "Can you hang out and have some?"

Sid shook his head. "Jimmy's coming in late, so it's pretty tight back there."

"You need a hand?"

"Probably not," Sid said. "But I'll let you know." He saw Buddy coming back. "Okay, okay, just tell me *which* ones you played."

" 'California Girls' — "

"*Naturally*," Sid said.

"And 'I Get Around.' "

"Boring," Sid said, heading back to the kitchen. "Very, very boring."

"I also put on Eddie Floyd and John Cougar Mellencamp," Buddy called after him.

Sid paused. "Which Johnny Cougar?"

" 'Crumblin' Down.' "

"Okay, you're forgiven." Sid went behind the counter. "*This* time."

"I Get Around" started playing. Loudly.

"It *is* a great song," Buddy said, sitting down to eat.

Charles shrugged, taking a piece of pizza. "At least it'll make me forget 'Mares-eat-oats.' "

"Aw, rats," Buddy said. "I'd finally managed to get it out of my head."

"Started up again?"

Buddy sighed. "Yeah." He stopped in the act of taking a bite of pizza. "Hey, check it out!"

"What?" Charles asked, looking around.

"Over there." Buddy nodded across the restaurant. "There's the girl I've been telling you about — isn't she great?"

Charles followed his gaze, seeing — he choked on his drink — Rachel. "Tell me you don't mean the one in the green sweater," he said, trying to get his breath back after choking.

Buddy hadn't even noticed. "Yeah — isn't she pretty? I should go over and talk to her, right?"

"Talk to Rachel," Charles said.

"Well, yeah, I — wait a minute, how'd you — " Buddy stopped, catching on. "Oh, no."

"Oh, *yes*," Charles said.

"Oh, no." Then Buddy narrowed his eyes. "No *wonder* she said she was busy Friday night."

Charles pushed his pizza away, his appetite gone. "Well, if you'd ever told me her *name*, Buddy, I wouldn't have — "

"*You* never told me her name, either," Buddy pointed out. "It's not like I — oh, no, she just got up! What do we do?"

Charles sighed. "Can we make it to the door?"

Buddy shook his head. "Not in time. Besides — look, she's just going up to the counter — she might not even notice us."

They watched her ask Sid something, then watched him reach under the counter, handing her a stack of napkins. As she walked back toward her table, she saw Charles and stopped.

"Hi, Charles," she said, smiling. "What are you — " She saw Buddy, too. "Buddy," she said, sounding very surprised. "Hi."

They both nodded, somewhat flushed.

"Do, um," she shifted her weight, also uncomfortable, "you guys know each other?"

"No," Buddy said grimly.

"Never met him," Charles said, just as grim.

Rachel let out her breath. "Oh, boy." She looked over at her friends. "Um, look, I'm just going to — I'll be right back, okay? I mean — don't leave or anything."

They watched her hurry over to her table.

"Do we take off?" Buddy asked.

Charles shook his head. "We're already humiliated enough."

Rachel came back over, holding a can of soda, from which she took a nervous sip.

"Your friends think this was pretty funny?" Buddy asked, gesturing with his head.

"No, I didn't — I mean, it *is* kind of funny," she said, "but — "

They both scowled.

"Mildly," she said, then hesitated. "Is it okay if I sit down?"

They both shrugged, each gesturing for her to sit with the other one. Instead, she turned to get a chair, pulling it up to the end of the table and sitting in it.

"Well," she said.

They both looked at her, folding their arms at the same time.

"I never noticed it," she said, "but you *are* a lot alike."

Neither of them smiled.

"So I guess you date more than one person at a time," Buddy said stiffly.

"What, Buddy, you wouldn't date two girls at the same time?" she asked. "Come on."

"Not if they *knew* each other!"

"I didn't *know* you knew each other," she said.

Charles nodded, starting to be a little amused by all of this. "She has a point, Buddy. I mean, it's a pretty big campus."

Rachel nodded, too. "Exactly. I mean, I like both of you, and when you asked me out — " Her smile was shy. "Well, I'll tell you, it made my day. I mean, *two* nice guys asking me out in *one* day — *well*. I even called home."

Charles laughed, forgetting to keep his arms folded. "Seriously?"

"Yeah," she said, also laughing. "I mean, I don't know about you guys, but that's a pretty good day for me."

Charles and Buddy looked at each other.

"That's a pretty good day for us, too," Buddy said.

Charles picked up his pizza, his appetite having returned a little. "A *very* good day."

Buddy nodded, picking up his own pizza. "Red-letter."

Joining in the spirit of things, Rachel

drank some of her soda. "So, what happens now?"

Buddy's posture stiffened. "I guess you have to choose," he said.

"*Choose?*" Charles shook his head. "Or what, Buddy? We go out and fight a duel?"

"She must like *one* of us better, Charles," Buddy said defensively. "She just has to tell us."

"No, I like both of you," Rachel said. "I'm not going to turn around and choose — that would be stupid."

"Okay, but, I'm not — " Charles paused, not sure what he wanted to say, or how he wanted to say it. "I don't know what the solution is," he said finally.

She grinned. "Well, this may sound pretty radical, but couldn't we be — friends?"

"*Friends?*" Buddy said, as though he had never heard the word before.

She nodded. "Yeah. I mean, I like you guys, you like each other, presumably you both like me — doesn't it seem like we could maybe work something out there?"

"Oh," Buddy said, frowning. "You mean, like — friends."

Charles and Rachel both laughed.

"Do you think that sounds okay?" Rachel asked. "Like a good idea?"

Charles sighed. Then Buddy sighed.

"Sure," Charles said.

"Why not," Buddy said.

It was quiet for a minute, a silence that managed to be both awkward and amusing.

Then, noticing the girls waiting impatiently at her table, Charles gestured over there.

"They look like they're ready to leave," he said.

Rachel glanced over, and nodded. "Yeah, they do. I should probably — " She hesitated. "You guys aren't mad at me, are you?"

"It was a misunderstanding," Charles said.

"Could happen to anyone," Buddy said.

"Okay." She nodded to her friends that she would be there in a minute, but still hesitated at the table. "Look, um — you guys want to go to the football game on Saturday? I mean, us and whoever else we can think of?"

Charles and Buddy looked at each other.

"Sure," Buddy said.

"Why not," Charles said.

When she and her friends had gone, they looked at each other again.

"Well," Charles said. "Is that the most embarrassing thing that's happened to you all week?"

"All *year*," Buddy said.

They both slouched down, looking at the now-cold pizza.

"Rats," Buddy said finally.

Charles nodded. "Double rats."

"I'm going to go put on all the Beach Boys songs that thing has," Buddy said.

Charles nodded, handing him a couple of quarters. "Please do."

They *did* all go to the football game on

Saturday. They had fun, even. Charles brought the Powell kids, Buddy dragged some guys from the dorm along, Rachel brought a couple of *her* friends. In fact, Buddy's friend Sam and Rachel's friend Polly hit it off, leaving after the game with the proverbial stars in their eyes. Charles and Buddy found this all the more depressing.

Since they were, in fact, dateless that night — and not in the mood to rectify the situation — they decided to go to Sid's and drown their sorrows in a Sid's Special.

Sid saw them and came right over to their table. "Hey, guys, what's up?"

"Hi, Sid," Charles said.

"Hi," Buddy said, with just as little energy.

Sid sat down. "Rough day?"

"*Terrible* day," Buddy said.

"No, it wasn't that terrible," Charles disagreed. "It was just — frustrating."

"Depressing," Buddy said.

"Women trouble?" Sid guessed.

They both nodded.

"Want me to put the 'No Love Songs' sign on the jukebox?"

They both nodded.

"Would an Extra Special with sliced meatballs, onions, walnuts, and sun-dried tomatoes cheer you up?"

"Very much," Charles said.

"Absolutely," Buddy said.

Sid got up. "Consider it done." He went over to the jukebox, taping the neat but emphatic NO LOVE SONGS TONIGHT sign above the selection buttons. Then, he dropped a quarter into the machine, punching in two songs. As he headed for the kitchen, the Beach Boys' "Surfin' U.S.A." started playing.

"You're a jewel, Sid!" Buddy yelled.

"I know!" Sid yelled back. "Spread it around."

They listened to the song without speaking for a minute.

"I really liked her," Buddy said. "Not as a friend, I mean."

Charles nodded. "Me, too."

"This is *serious* Sophomore Slump."

"I'd say so, yeah," Charles agreed.

They didn't say anything, Buddy taking a napkin and idly tearing it into pieces, Charles twirling the hot pepper flakes shaker.

"This is a great *song*, anyway," Buddy said.

Charles laughed. "I've heard worse."

They listened to the end of the song, then Twisted Sister's "We're Not Gonna Take It" came on. From the kitchen, they could hear Sid laughing at his own humor.

"Nice one!" Charles yelled to him.

"Inspirational, I thought!" Sid yelled back.

They were drinking their sodas and waiting for the pizza when the restaurant door opened, two vaguely familiar-looking girls coming in. They were both very pretty, but also wholesome sorts, one with short blonde hair, the other with shoulder-length dark hair.

"I bet they have boyfriends," Buddy said glumly.

Charles nodded. "I bet they do, too."

But, passing their table, one of the girls paused.

"Hey, aren't you guys in our Abnormal Psychology class?" she asked.

That must be why they looked familiar. "Uh, yeah," Charles said. "I guess we are."

The other girl stopped, too. "Is it true she actually made a pie?"

"You heard about that?" Charles said, tempted to give Buddy a good, hard kick under the table.

"I think the whole class heard about it," the first girl said.

"It was very *good* pie," Buddy said. "I mean, she brought us in a couple of pieces."

The girls laughed.

"I guess it's a good thing she has a sense of humor," one of them said.

"*Very* good," Charles said, lowering an eyebrow at Buddy, who looked innocent.

"Very *lucky*," the other girl said, laughing.

"Wait a minute," Buddy got up as they started to leave. "Are you two meeting anyone here?"

The girls exchanged glances.

"Well — no," one of them said, "but — "

"Would you care to join us?" Buddy asked, with his Mr. Charming smile.

The girls hesitated.

"Well — " one of them started.

Charles got up, too. "We'd really like it if you did," he said, trying for a Mr. Charming smile, but ended up, he suspected, with a Mr. Sincere one.

The girls looked at each other again, then shrugged affirmatively.

"Sure," one of them said.

"Why not," the other one said.

Buddy moved to let them sit down. "I'm Buddy, and that's my friend, Charles."

"I'm Beth, and that's my friend, Laurie," the girl with dark hair said.

They all nodded at each other and then, as the girls sat down, Buddy grinned across the table at him, Charles having to grin back.

Maybe things were going to be okay, after all.